THE LAST BOOKSTORE

BROOKE PURDY AND COLETTE FREEDMAN

"You can be a hero in an age of none."

– The Clash

DEDICATION

This is for Max and Scout—my "reasons."
Stay true, stay bold, stay brave. Always choose love.
Know that you hold LIONHEARTED courage and
boundless creativity. Whenever I am too small, you build
me. When I am beaten down by doubt and "life," you
boost me. You inspire me. Every single day, in a
thousand ways I never imagined possible.
But mostly you make me feel. All the feelings.
Sometimes so big I feel like I will collapse under their
immensity. I tried to contain some of them here.
Just know that every word, every feeling, the bravery,
heart, and love of all of the characters… is you.
I love you with everything I have.
Dream big.

To my extraordinary nephews, Zac and Dylan.
You are my heart.

It wasn't zombies.

My mom and dad say it was Man. The heart-still-beating kind. To make a long story short—and this is from my parents—who heard the stories from their parents—who were there when it happened—with all of them probably editing out the real gruesome stuff—it was what they call an EMP. That's like this huge wave of electric energy blasted at us like a laser.

It blew out all our power. Everywhere.

The attacks were coordinated. As in, they blasted us and a bunch of other countries from ships on the ocean and blew up our power grid. Everything electronic. Everything. They called it "the Darkening." I guess at that time, people were pretty into their electricity because it all went to crap after that. When all the power went out, a lot of people freaked out. Some tried to run away, some tried to wait it out, some tried to fix it, but most people just lost it. Dad says most of the population had no idea about basic survival.

The worst, though, were the "Blighters"—well, that's what they're known as now. They saw the Darkening as a way to take. And they took and they burned and they killed. Mom says the world could have recovered if everyone hadn't freaked out and the Blighters hadn't taken control of the cities. She says the "good people" could have fought back. But they never organized... and then it was too late. The Blighters seized control. It's okay enough for us, though, because we're "Landers." We live out in the farm country and stay far enough away from the old cities to avoid any problems. We built a wall. We keep away.

We mind our own business and we stay alive.

– Jack Weller, Age 14

Chapter One
Jack

"First tap!" I yell.

"Nope. I had that!" Logan's red hair is the first to emerge from the brush. He's the tallest and the oldest of us at fourteen and a half. He's also my best friend. "Yep, me, definitely me."

We've been playing Tap for as long as I can remember. We line up old cans from before the Darkening, because no one makes cans anymore. I don't even know what "soda" tastes like, but it sounds like it might have been great. On "three" we stand and rapid fire at them with our slingshots. Logan always wins. Always. Well, unless we let Beckett play.

Beckett's my little sister—she's twelve but she acts like she's twenty. She also has the best natural aim I've ever seen. She's the only one who can beat Logan three games straight, so Logan doesn't like when she plays. Today we ditched her, and I'll probably pay for that later.

Still holding our slingshots, Digits, Mateo, and I pop our heads out and I'm still pretty sure I was first tap. "C'mon, this is all me." I bend down and examine the can. "Right, Mateo?"

Mateo's parents are best friends with my parents, so he has to get my back. He's a year younger than I am, but for a thirteen-year-old he's pretty hefty and definitely the strongest guy I know. He's also the most talkative. If I'm ever in a bad mood, he's the guy I wanna hang out with. He can make anyone laugh—if you don't try and throttle him first.

But Mateo is just standing there, looking at the only can still on the fence. "So, wait, it's not me, then?"

"Mateo, you aim like a goat," Logan tells him as he starts collecting the ammo.

"Like a goat with mittens," I say as I grab my blue ammo.

Mats won't give up, though. "This was mine, right, Digits?"

Digits is Logan's little brother. His real name is Gideon—but we all call him Digits on account of him signing with his fingers. He caught a bad cold when he was little, like age four, and has been deaf ever since. I honestly don't even remember him ever talking—we've just always signed with him. Even though he's only eleven and the smallest, I'm pretty sure he's a genius... I know, because I've tried to argue with him. It's a losing game.

Digits signs to Mateo. We all crack up.

"What? What did he say?" Even though we've all been taught how to sign since Digits went deaf, Mateo is... challenged at it sometimes. Thankfully, Digits can read a mouth from twenty yards out.

"He said that you aim like a goat with mittens, glasses, and a twitch," Logan interprets for him.

"I HIT THAT COKE CAN!" Mateo insists.

He's determined, I'll give him that. Logan's rocks are red, mine are blue, Digits's are green, and Mateo's are yellow. Let's just say that we don't see a lot of yellow marks on cans. When we let her play, Beckett's rocks are rainbow because . . . girls.

I check the cans. "None of the cans are marked with yellow, Mats. Sorry. I'm telling you, mine was first tap—see that blue there?"

Logan just smiles. Damn, that hair—bugs me sometimes.

Digits hands Mateo the pile of yellow rocks.

Mateo clumsily signs, "Fine. I get it, Digits." He doesn't even have control of his fingers, much less his aim.

I'm the one to break it to him. "You just said, 'Hurt, shovel,' Mats."

"C'mon, Jack. I hit at least one, right?"

"You're definitely getting better."

Mateo gets all flustered and kicks a can at Logan. Logan dodges it, and it's on. We start kicking and dribbling the can toward the Old Road, which is more like a big dirt path since only horses and bikes travel on it. I guess I'm still kinda irritated about first tap and I kick it really hard . . . kinda at Logan. He dodges it and it bangs across the road into the gully.

Natch.

They all look at me since it was my kick. I pocket my ammo and go to get it. I walk down toward the gully at the forest's edge and take a deep breath because I know what's coming. Of course, the can is right under one of them, and the bones are super old. Dried out and white. It's hard not to think about how these used to be people. My mom says so many died around Lander's End that eventually they just stopped cleaning up the bodies, shoved them off to the sides, and told us not to go there.

But we know.

I can hear the guys messing around as I get a stick and try to poke the can away from the skeleton. I just focus on the can. If you squint, though, it looks like a crazy kind of wheat field.

Of the dead.

Chapter Two
Beckett

Jack. Is. Dead.

He thinks he's SO smart—telling me that Mom wanted to meet me in town, which usually means maple candy. I rode all the way there and stood around for, like, AN HOUR before I realized what had happened.

Jack and his mucker friends just can't handle the fact that I'm the best shot of all of them… cause I'm a GIRL. I mean, of all the totally stupid, useless reasons to be jealous… Listen, I wish I could write my name in the dirt with pee, but ya don't see ME blaming everybody else cause I can't.

So they went off and played their damn Tap by themselves. Fine.

He'll pay. I've been collecting Franklin's turds for the past half hour. Franklin is one of our horses— he's super old. Dad calls his poop "road apples," which I think is the nastiest thing ever AND totally inaccurate cause they look nothing like any apples I've ever seen.

So, I'm gonna nail Jack with them until he is covered in old Franklin turd… Maybe then he'll think twice about ditching me. Even though, as far as big brothers go, he's pretty okay. Nava's big brother pours freezing water on her EVERY morning, so I know Jack isn't so bad. Nava does snore, though.

Mom said I had to get to my chores, so I've been hiding from her since I got home. There's like eight million chores and it's not fair. We live on a big farm. We get our own water from a cistern and well. Our windmill powers what little stuff we have, like the shortwave radio and a light here or there that didn't get fried in the Darkening. Solar panels everywhere help with the rest. Batteries work still, but those are in short supply and high demand. You gotta trade a cow or something for two. We also have a million animals. Horses, sheep, goats, chickens, three cats, two dogs, and a peacock who wanders off for a week at a time but always comes back.

So, that adds up to a lot of damn chores. Every day. I think this is completely unfair, though, because I know that back in the old days, people like Grandma and Grandpa had robots and machines and all kinds of things that did everything FOR them. They just sat around and played VIDEO GAMES.

I would give all my Tap ammo for a chance to play VIDEO GAMES.

Jack has to come in this way and there's no cover. It's a trap. I got him. I piled up all my horse turds in a huge pile by our front fence. I also have a backup stash by the front door because as soon as he spots me... he's gonna go for me. I'll run there and BAM—second trap.

He's coming and I aim. PERFECT shot. Hits him right in the cheek!

"Beckett! You are so done!" Jack screams as he runs after me into the house. NATCH! I'm running. Too fast. Forget the backup pile. GOTTA GET TO MOM.

"I'm gonna kill you, Beckett!" Jack screams at my back. I'm twisty—he can't grab on yet.

"Not if you can't catch me!" I yell back as I run through our front door and dive under our big wood table.

6

"Mommommom, Jack's gonna kill me!"

"Get OFF ME!" He has my legs. I squirm, I kick, I buck. Nothing. He has me.

"Say 'knock.'" Jack grins, pinning me. Stupid fatty.

"Nope… Oh, and you got a bunch of FRANKLIN POO ON YOUR CHEEK." I manage to twist out from under the goocher as he tries to wipe the poop off. Just in time, my mom walks in. I run behind her.

"You guys, quit." My mom's using her unnaturally calm voice. You need to listen when she uses the unnaturally calm voice. Dad says it's "the signal to the storm." I'm holding her by the waist, putting her between poop-face Jack and me, and she seems… smaller. Like, I can feel her ribs. I mean, she's always been tall and not at all fat, but she's just… less. Like she might break. I let go and step back. I don't wanna feel her bones. She sits on the couch. I don't want her to sit either.

"She nailed me with turds again, Mom!" Jack whines. I suddenly don't care if he catches me. But he just stands there.

"Becks, don't throw turds at your brother," Mom says. "And you might want to wash your face." She looks at me, and her face has this little glint. The corner of her mouth turns up just a tiny bit. She's trying not to laugh.

There she is. I smile back at her. She goes back to "serious mom."

"Beckett, you hear me?"

"It was just one." A GREAT one. Big, fresh, and from all the way across the pigpen, too.

"No more. Jack, go clean up," Mom says as she stands and goes back to the kitchen. Moving slower.

"So she can just get away with it?" Jack just doesn't know when to quit.

"You finish your chores?" she asks him over her shoulder. I stay close to her, just in case. I give Jack THE FACE and he instantly turns red. He's so easy. Always has been.

"Yes," Jack mumbles. See, I know for a FACT that his chores aren't done because I had to empty the compost for him. But Mom always knows when we're lying. Like, always. It's annoying. And kinda spooky.

"Really?" She looks at him with her super Mom sense.

"Well, most. But…" See, we always crack. But him sooner than me. Ha.

"Go." Mom stares at him, with his same blue-green eyes. I got my dad's eyes. They're more hazel. "Mystery eyes," Dad calls 'em.

Jack throws an episode and stomps out the door with his poo face. HA HA.

Mom catches me grinning. Gotta stop that. She uses that voice again. "Don't even start, Becks, and go wash your hands."

"But, Mom…" I follow her into our kitchen and wash my hands. I love our kitchen. It's not even as big as our main room, but somehow everyone always ends up here. It looks like a store. There are all of Mom's spices, herbs, and seasonings from the garden in these jars along one wall. There's a huge picture window that shines in all the sun for most of the day. It's warm here. Warm-feeling. You can hear the mini genie that powers our ice chest and the hum of the shortwave in the corner, and it kinda makes this room feel like it's… alive. Mom stands at our big iron stove and stirs something. My stomach growls. She hands me an apple without even looking at me. It looks nothing like a Franklin turd.

"Mom, I asked him to go shooting and he ditched me again! He and all his stupid friends. They're too scared to take me cuz plonker Logan knows I'm a better shot than he is."

"How about your chores?"

She's still stirring. I should probably taste it. My mom is the best cook in the world. Except for "Aunt" Willa, Mateo's mom. Willa makes a pie so good you wanna fight someone for it.

"Becks, chores?"

Damn. I was JUST thinking about PIE. "What about them?"

Mom turns around and stares at me with her "serious mom" face. Normally, I'd just give in and go do it. But her eyes… There're dark circles under them. They shouldn't be there. It makes me hot inside. Then… mad. "UGH! I HATE CHORES! All the time, every minute, chores. That's all I do. Always. I can't even do anything but chores!" Why do I have to do chores? Why can't I just hang out with Jack and his friends? Why do those BLACK CIRCLES sit on my MOM'S FACE!? I wanna kick something. "I mean, I am always doing chores! Feeding the pigs and the chickens and the rabbits and… and… and walking the horses and carrying hay

9

and…and…and making my bed! I mean, I am always doing chores!"

Mom breaks into a smile. "I know, it's horrible, right? How you guys are safe and well-fed and have to take care of the eight thousand animals you begged us to keep. It's awful. I mean, if I were you, I'd just run off to eat garbage with the Blighters. Now *that's* living. Stupid chores. In fact…"

She stops cooking and starts doing an imitation of… well, me, I guess. Needs work if ya ask me. "I CAN'T BELIEVE HOW UNFAIR IT IS! I HATE COOKING AND EATING AND SLEEPING IN A WARM BED!" Now she's on the ground, waving her arms around and kicking—it's actually kinda funny, but I am NOT going to smile. She keeps going. "UGH, I HATE IT—I WISH I COULD JUST HANG OUT AND THROW TURDS AT MY BROTHER! WHY CAN'T I JUST THROW TURDS!!?"

DANG. I can't help it. A smile pops outta my face. I whip a hand up to hide it, but she already saw. She grins back. I want to stay. I have this sudden weird urge to just crawl onto her lap, right there on the kitchen floor.

"What's all this?"

My dad. He and my mom are pretty much the most in love, strangest, greatest married people ever. He's handsome too—I mean, for a dad. It helps that when he smiles, he does it with his eyes too. They shine and crinkle and make you smile back just because. He's doing that to my mom right now. He hugs me from the back and goes to help her up. Why does she need help?

"What's the matter? You want to throw turds again, honey?" He kisses her head. The circles under her eyes seem lighter. Can love do that?

"Yep. All day." Mom smiles at him. Seems like they talk in their heads to each other. Telepathic. YES, I know, big words. Jack isn't the only one who reads around here. Mom kisses him back. It's small. Shouldn't be anything different, but my eyes start stinging.

"Fine. I'll do my janky chores," I stand and announce. Just to break the eye-sting thing. "But it's not fair that there used to be ROBOTS before the Darkening and now there're NONE. Or video games. Now I'm your robot. Stupid Darkening. When Aunt Willa brings her pie over tonight, I'M GONNA LICK THE WHOLE TOP, then eat the whole DANG THING."

I gotta get out of here. My perfect kitchen seems too bright. Dad's hands are too gentle on Mom's waist. Her kiss was too sweet. I have to get out.

I slam the door behind me.

Chapter Three
Mateo

DAMN Beckett!

See, i had, like, this strategy, right? It was 2 let her win a little, then i'd pounce an' make her sorry 4 challenging me 2 a Turbo War game. It started out great. Only thing is… i can't really count the cards like i thought. i think only Digits can do that—that's why no one ever plays with him. Plus, Beckett's still all mad at us 4 ditching her 2day.

Damn girls.

My mom an' dad are downstairs with Uncle Reese an' Aunt Avery, Jack and Beckett's parents. They're talking all low. Grownup talk. We usually eat at each other's houses once or twice a week. We're pretty much like family. Tho Beckett isn't acting very sisterly or whatever. Greedy, really. But Jack's all quiet. Can't get him 2 go play Hay Dive or anything. He just wants 2 stay upstairs in the loft an' listen 2 the grownups without them knowing.

"That's like the 7th ace, Becks!" How can she have all the aces? Plus, she had like 4 slices of pie. Greedy.

Jack keeps shushing me, but that's normal. Sometimes he gets all thinky an' quietlike. i try an' wait til he's thought whatever he needs 2, but i just got a lot 2 say sometimes.

"HA! Got 1. Brace 4 my COMEBACK!" i whisper-yell at Becks.

"Shhhh! Mats!" Jack again. His face is pushed almost alla way through the dang stair posts.

"We'll call it a draw," Beckett says as she scoots up next 2 Jack 2 listen.

"But you have like ALL my—"

"Shhh!" Both of 'em. Maybe this is a plan they had.

"Hey, are you guys working 2gether an'—"

"Mats! Just can it 4 a minute!" Jack's face is super serious, so i try. Hard. What's so interesting down there anyway? Their talks are usually about farming (BORING) or town business (DOUBLE BORING), or sometimes they're all happy an' silly (EMBARRASSING) an' talk about the "old days," be4 the Darkening stuff.

i look over Jack's shoulder. My mom's listening 2 Aunt Avery's chest. She hasn't been feeling well an' my mom's been helping. She's like the closest thing 2 a doctor that Lander's End has, an' she has all these herbs an' leaves an' medicine-like plants that—

WHOA.

Aunt Avery's ribs an' back—what I can see anyway—are all covered in dark red an' purple bruises.

This is bad.

"How are the ribs?" My mom is being very gentle, but her 4head's all scrunched. It's her "doctor face."

"The breathing is harder at night. My joints are… okay." Aunt Avery seems like she's trying 2 be less sick. Those bruises, tho… i see my dad an' Uncle Reese trying 2 be okay.

But i know.

It's the same stuff i saw my mom trying 2 fix with Frank Dunner an' his wife, Crabby Junie. Guess that's disrespectful, tho, since they died. That was last month. The Batemans died the month be4 that, an' Old Man McFeely last winter. They all had those same bruises. Mom says that a while ago a lot of people died cause we don't have the "old medicine" that people used 2 have. Mom has her "lab," tho. She reads all these old medical books that everyone brings her. She mixes an' cooks an' tries all these concoctions an' stuff 2 help. Sometimes she accidentally blows stuff up in there an' that's the gravy part, if ya ask me. Some of the stuff works. Some doesn't.

The stuff 4 the Dunners, the Batemans, an' Old Man McFeely... didn't. My mom doesn't sleep much these days. She also cries sometimes when she thinks everyone's asleep. i feel bad 4 her.

And the dead folks.

Beckett is crying. Not like baby crying, but the super sad kind, where tears just fall off her nose. i hate it. i don't know what 2 do. i'd give her some of my ammo 2 try an' cheer her up, but she already took it all.

"Is it the Bleeds?" Uncle Reese is holding Aunt Avery's hand. He's talking 2 my mom, but he an' Aunt Avery are just staring at each other. Jack's shoulders are up around his ears. Beckett is pouring tears an' my dad is pacing.

"It's okay, honey. I'll be okay." Aunt Avery's tryin' 2 be brave, but i know when someone's faking. Like when you get hit hard in front of a girl. All you wanna do is cry, but don't you dare.

My mom gets all doctory. "Look, it seems similar—but I don't know. We've had 6 cases this season alone. I'm doing my best but I only have the knowledge from the texts I'm able 2 scavenge. If I had a better working knowledge of the old antibiotics and medicines, I could possibly work up a natural mimic, but…"

She stops talking. i hate seeing my mom like this. Helpless.

Uncle Reese stands up, real sudden. "So I'll go county 2 county. Ask on the shortwave… I can—"

"We've already done that, Reese." Finally. My Dad pipes up. He's real good in tough spots. i've watched him tame a wild pig just by looking at 'em in his way. He's talking 2 Reese now—like friend 2 friend. "We've scoured every Lander within 30 miles."

But Uncle Reese is looking all trapped, like when you corner a barn rat. "Could it fix it? Stop it? The right information?" He's talking 2 my mom.

i wanna shout at her, "Fix it, MOM!" Just so Beckett'll stop crying an' i won't see Jack's shoulders shake no more.

"You guys wanna go…" i try. Anything. They don't even bother 2 shush me. THAT'S bad.

They just focus on my mom, who is still inspecting Aunt Avery's arms and legs—they're all covered in bruises. Mom turns 2 Uncle Reese. "Of course, more information might help, but I can't guarantee it. 50 years ago, this would have been a simple office visit and prescription. Now, we're getting beat down by influenza 4 Chrissake. I can't…"

If my MOM starts crying, i'm gonna break something.

"What about the old hospitals?" Uncle Reese says, that wild look growing. He's walking in circles.

15

Good, my mom has her "doctor face" on again. No crying right now. "The medication was either wiped out by Blighters or expired. The EMPs fried the pharmaceutical plants and practically everything else." She's talking 2 him but it doesn't look like he's listening.

"Medical journals? Notes? Come on, there must be something. Anything." His voice is louder but sounds like it might break or something.

My dad tries 2 calm him. "Reese, they're all in the middle of war zones. It's a death sentence."

Uncle Reese spins around an' points at Aunt Avery. "And what is this, Garrett?!"

Aunt Avery lets out a sound. It's a crying sound but reminds me of 1 of the sheep, like when it's scared. Bleating.

Both Jack an' Beckett make these weird sounds an' i wanna CRUSH SOMETHING. Beckett is full-tilt crying now, her body shaking, her face all red. Jack slaps a hand over her mouth. "Shhh. Follow me."

Jack heads in2 their room an' i see where he's going.

BALLS.

i suck it up, tho. They're going out on their roof. i hate it up there! It's all slope-y an' steep, an' there's just black sky all around. Fine. i follow cause nothing about this night is normal. Maybe if we go out here, it'll feel a little more regular… at least 4 them. Man, i can be a great guy sometimes. i should get my ammo back 4 this. i step out super slow an' lie on my back, close 2 the house. This is the only way i can do it.

It's super quiet. Unless they can hear my heart about 2 explode. That, an' Beckett's sniffling. Dang, i hate this. Everything is crap, crap, crap.

i wanna say a thousand things. i can feel all the words up in my throat, like barf about 2 just explode out, but i stop.

Beckett seems 2 calm down a little. "We have 2 fix her," she says 2 Jack, who wipes away a tear, an' i swear in that moment that i will NEVER judge him 4 it. My heart is slowing down, but it's hurting so bad 4 him.

"Becks, we can't! You heard! It's the Bleeds. She needs medicine that doesn't even exist!" Jack's half yelling but nobody holds it against him. Wish he'd quit wavin' his damn arms around, tho.

It's quiet 4 a while. Seems like 2 hours but it's prolly only about 20 seconds. i don't do real good with quiet.

Alla sudden, i have the greatest mind-EXPLODING thought ever. There's a word 4 it—but that's Jack's an' Digits's department. They're word guys.

"Jack, what about Logan's story? About the bookstore…" i'm trying 2 sound calm but—seriously? MIND. EXPLOSION. THING.

"No."

Maybe he didn't hear me, so i keep calm. "You know, how Logan says his cousin knew about it? A way in? We could—"

"No."

Natch that. i keep talking. This is the best idea i've ever had. The best idea anyone's ever had. "We could go there an' get a book? Like, with medicine

formulas or whatever. His cousin said it was FILLED
with all kinds of—"

Jack suddenly stands up ON THE TILTED
ROOF. "It's in Armor City. It's Blighter territory. Also,
it's a MYTH!"

My exploding mind is currently at war with my
friend-flying-off-a-roof thoughts. It's that bad quiet
again. i wanna argue so bad it's burning me.

"Jack, if we don't help… who will?" Beckett
speaks up, but quiet. She's really serious.

Jack looks at her, just as serious. They stare at
each other in that way that you know they are "talking"
still. "I dunno, Becks. But I can't see how both of us
getting killed is gonna help either. We… we should go 2
bed."

He starts back inside the house. Becks starts 2
follow him. What about me?
WAITWAITWAITWAITWAITWAITWAIT!

"Uhhh…" i manage 2 choke out. "Filled with
terror. Total terror." i think i'd pee my pants if anything
worked right. Beckett leans down an' takes my hand an'
leads me in. Any other time, this would be embarrassing,
but not half as much as wetting my pants. i take it an'
stand. Looking only at the window. NOT anywhere else.
i reach safety an' collapse.

And just like that, i don't give 2 craps about my
ammo anymore.

Chapter Four
Logan

Jankiest. Idea. Ever.

Look, I know Jack is smart, almost as smart as Digits, but... come on. Even though he can't throw for crap, he's a super smart guy, and I'd say that even if he weren't my best friend. But this? I mean, first he steals Beckett's bike, which is just asking for it. She's going to find out and, well, that girl can be damn stubborn. She's going to follow us to the ends of the Wall to get him back for that.

The part that really gets me is that this whole plan was brought up by <u>Mateo</u>. If you ask me, that's like following a bug to find a water source. Slow and just... silly. I've seen the guy get outsmarted by a branch. But I won't even talk about this with Jack. First off, right now he's got that "look." I've seen it millions of times. Mostly when we're wrestling or he's trying to beat me at something. It's all cold and... well, you might as well just go with it cause you're not going to shake it off him til he's done. But also... this is for his <u>mom</u>. I mean, she's... not doing good. Also, well, to be honest, I've never been out of Lander's. There's an entire world outside the Wall, and if I can get a chance to see it <u>and</u> help save Jack's mom, I'll take it. Plus, I'm no wailer, gotta brace up.

So here we are. Standing in the middle of Main Street, which is the only street with a real name in our town since all the stores are on it—ya know, like a blacksmith, a mercantile, a general goods, ya know, normal stuff. At the end of the street is the garage/small-motors shop, which brings me to what steams me most about the whole thing.

Badger.

I guess he's my "cousin," but if we share any of the same blood, I won't claim it, and no one's been able to really break it down, so… he's just Badger. He's been the town's goocher since he was born. Not just thick in the head but also usually leaning toward mean. "Nothing worse than ignorant AND ornery," says my pa. When Digits and I were smaller, Badger used to chase us with lizards and try to put 'em down our shirts.

Then we got bigger. And started liking lizards. Total. Goocher.

Anyway, for this whole crazy plan to work, we need him. So I go in first and the rest of them follow. Before the Darkening, people used to drive cars. I would trade anything to get to drive a car like I've seen in books or the old mags. Anyway, garages were for them, and since they don't work anymore, this place is mostly for repair on small motors that folks have built themselves. They fix and sell bike motors, genie motors, shortwave radios, regulators, stuff like that. I don't even know how Badger got to work here. He's like a fly in the jelly. Good for nothing and a waste of… good jelly. He sees us, lifts his welding mask, and glares. He clangs his iron hammer down real loud. Guess we're supposed to be scared. What a clown.

"What's up, young bloods?"

He even talks like an idiot. He's only ten years older than I am and he thinks he's got some kinda say over me. He doesn't. I've got this lame smile on my face like I think he's funny when all I wanna do is punch him.

Center mass. I glance at Jack and he's got the same smile. See? Smart. He once said that Badger was "stupid as a goose fart" and I laughed so hard I almost threw up.

So, Goose Fart unties his leather apron like he's gonna go on a break and keeps on talking. "You can forget gettin' any 'plosives, Logan. Almost got beat after you guys blew up the pig trough. Dick nuggets." I didn't even blow the damn thing up. <u>He</u> did. Goocher.

Digits signs, "Goose fart," and I gotta bite the inside of my cheek so hard cause I'm about to burst out laughing. I can't even look toward Jack.

Badger's face, with his disgusting four teeth in it, gets all red. He gets up in Digits's face. "Listen, butt munch, I don't read fingers." He makes some wild finger motions then ends with his middle finger. Damn, if Jack didn't need this so badly, I'd knock Badger flat.

Mateo distracts me from my hate by laughing. "You just told Digits to 'listen.'" Sometimes, I want to hug that guy... when I don't wanna deck him.

"You shut the hell up too, Tubby Bubble," Badger growls. This is goin' south. Mateo, for once, shuts up and raises his hands, giving up.

Badger calms down a bit. I know his tiny brain can't take much more. "Look, Badge, we need you to tell us everything you know about the Last Bookstore."

Soon as he hears me say it, I see something spread across his face. Fear? I mean, it was real fast and then he wiped it off real quick. But I swear he just looked terrified.

Then he's back. "Why? Books are busted."

Jack steps forward, simple smile still in place. He's good. "Please, Badger. It's really important."

21

Badger is just sneering that ugly face. I can't do this anymore.

"His mom's got the Bleeds," I blurt. I don't know if any of us have said that out loud yet. We've all known since yesterday, but we haven't said the <u>word</u>. Like, to say it would open up some badness. More badness.

Badger, if you can believe it, gets kind of serious. Well, serious as a goose fart can get. "So what? You wanna read? What the hell, books are like television, son. Extinct."

We read about television in school. Badger knows it from stories. Seemed like the most gravy thing ever, except for cars. Jack ignores how stupid Badger is and keeps talking. "Look, what do you want? For all the info you have?"

Jack lets Badger think. But we planned this. We know what's coming… eventually. Finally, a slow, evil grin creeps over Badger's face, like a worm twisting outta the mud. I sneak a look at Jack. He gets all serious. Dang, he's good.

"No way," Jack says, shaking his head. I almost believe him myself. Wonder if I could act that good?

"But wait, that's—" Mateo starts. Digits slaps his hand then fakes like it was a fly. Natch. Mateo's gonna blow it, and we explained the plan like four times!

I jump in. "THAT'S way too much to ask. He loves that bike, Badger." Ha! Maybe I <u>am</u> as good as Jack. Mateo shuts up.

See, this is why Jack stole Beckett's bike. It's the best bike in Lander's. Beckett and her dad have been snazzing it up for about two years—fat tires, new spokes, clean motor. Our rides are okay, but she loves hers like a pet. Even named it—"Oliver." Don't ask.

Jack sticks to his part. "Is there anything else you'd want?" He looks super sad.

Badger steps up—here we go. "You got tobacco?" Jack shakes his head no. "Liquor?" Another no from Jack. "Batteries? Wiring? Copper?" No. No. No. "Y'all are as useless as a hat fulla busted assholes." Goose Fart strikes again. I can see Mateo out of the corner of my eye, trying to figure out this last gem as Jack sighs this real sad sigh and finally… rolls the bike over to Badger, who grins like he won something and starts checking it out. No one says anything. We could be on fire for all he cares.

"Uhhh, Badge?" We've gotta get the information and get out of here. There's a lot we have to do before we head out tomorrow. And even though we are about to leave a town we've never left our whole lives, honestly… I'm most scared of Beckett. NOT that I'm scared of a girl but… if I were… it would be her, with a head full of revenge and no bike. The only reason we were even able to snatch it was because Jack's dad has been working on it and she's been getting rides to school with him on his horse. Badger looks over his prize a couple seconds more, then stashes it in the garage. Suddenly, I feel all bad for Oliver—but worse for Jack.

Becks is gonna kill him.

"Okay, listen up, muckers. I'm only gonna go through this once. I got this… thing and a—a kinda map, but you goochers ain't getting it. Plan on trading REAL goods for it someday. I'll just tell you what I know. And it's a lot."

23

Holy horse turds, Goose Fart has a map. I don't care if I'm begging. "Please, Badge. A map would really—"

He makes this sound, like a half laugh, half cough. What a plonker. "Hell. No. Here's one thing— Walberg found it back when we were in school—"

"Ha! You weren't never in—" Mateo gets out before Digits stomps on his foot. Mateo YELPS and Digits glares him quiet. For someone who can't talk, my brother can sure stare-speak about a million different feelings.

Badger sneers. "Okay, Lumpy, you're about to get nothing."

"Please, Badge," I say. "He didn't mean nothing. What do you have?" I think about how my voice sounds, and I'm gonna make Mats pay later for making me have to use this voice.

Badger stares at us for a minute—I think we're all holding our breath—then he pulls out his old homemade wallet, opens it, and pulls out this thin, papery-looking strip. It looks so old and worn I'm afraid to breathe on it. Like it might crumble. He turns it carefully toward us (seeing Badger handle anything with care like this is strange enough), and we can see it's a bookmark and it's got this old, fancy star on the top of it. I know from geography that it's the North Star. There're words too. Jack reads, "BOOKS, MAGAZINES, COLLECTIBLES" and part of an address: "80 CEDAR AVENUE." We just stare as Badger hands it to Jack, who takes it delicately. All the boys lean in, looking at it.

Of course, it's Mateo who ruins the moment. "Uhhh, you guys know that's just a bookmark, right? I mean, we make 'em in Ms. Gilroy's—"

I have to check him. "Mats! Shut up. That's not the point. It's from…" I'm scared to say it.

"The Last Bookstore," Jack whispers.

Badger, bein' all loud and stupid, busts in. "That's right. Word is, it's the last one in the whole territory that might still exist. So you goochers can have that and what's in here." He taps his pointy head and I almost burst out laughing again. We stare at him.

"Take it or leave it, muckers," he dares us. Just then, Digits starts signing to Jack with this tense look on his face. Jack shakes his head and they start to argue. I can feel what's coming. Before I can stop it, Badger grabs Digits by the collar. "What the natch! I told you all about them wiggly fingers—"

I'm about to smash him one when Jack steps up super fast. "Sorry, boss. He's just gotta go real bad." Man… I coulda blown the whole thing. Sometimes Jack has the coolest head—I run way faster than him, though.

"Dang, all's you gotta do is point at yer parts and I'd know," Badger says, pointing to his parts. Pretty sure he took a lotta blows to the head. "Through the shop—outhouse in back." Digits walks behind Badger as he starts to hold court. He stands in front of us like some kind of teacher. Janky ol' goose fart. But we are all still hanging on every word. This is why we are here. Even Mateo goes still.

"The Last Bookstore is in the middle of Armor City. Deep Blighter turf. Not one Lander I know that even got close ever walked away. 'Cept my friend Lonny. And he's talked all stuttery ever since."

Jack, Mats, and I kinda form this half circle around him to block his view of the shop and Digits. I can sorta see Digits searching silently through the shelves. Man, he can be quiet. I see him reach behind a box and hold up what looks like two homemade explosives. Jack nods but makes it look like he's doing it to Badger. Digits pockets the explosives as Badger talks faster, thinking he's the king of the hill right now.

Stupid goocher.

"See, Lonny found a way into the Underground, outside the Wall by the under-train tracks. I got his map, but you gotta know—once you cross the river, you're pretty much dead."

I'm nodding away, trying to copy Jack, but then I start to feel like I'm doing it too much so I stop. Digits is looking through the shelves again, and I can just feel time running out. Badger is gonna notice he's gone. I see Digits crawl under a shelf and open a box, looking through it. His eyes go all big and he holds up this really old-looking paper, all sparkly-eyed and nodding.

The MAP.

I can feel the three of us go super still an' stiff, trying not to let on how excited we are. All of us, staring so hard at Badger, no one blinking. Badger is just yammering away. "There's an old plumbing tunnel that runs from the under-train station right up under the bookstore. Lonny said you can get in and out without anyone knowing."

Digits pockets the map and joins up with us just as silent as ever. I hear Mateo let out a huge breath and almost wallop him. But I feel the same. That was close, and I feel like I wanna blink a thousand times right now.

Badger keeps going. "Now, see here—this musta been 'bout six years ago when Lonny went, but he said it was like no one had been inside since the Darkening. He tried to grab a buncha books but got caught by some of the Underfolk on his way back. He's never talked about it, but I dunno how he survived. Everyone knows the Underfolk are all cannibalians."

See, everyone doesn't really <u>know</u> this—it's just something everyone has always talked about. And yes, I KNOW, the word is cannibals. Jack isn't the only one to ever crack a book or listen in school. See, the Underfolk have been talked about as half demons, half people, or these ghost-white monsters who eat your bones, or snake-like scaly creatures with poison nails. It depends on who you talk to. All's I know is that I've had nightmares about them ever since I was little. Still do. I just don't talk about it. Gives me a shiver even now. I try and focus on Badger's stupid voice.

"The whole trip should take two days—if you haul ass and don't get eaten. Logan, if you say one word to anyone about me havin' or passin' on this info, I'll beat you so hard you'll go blind. Once you pass the Wall, though... if you see a soul, you run and don't stop, hear? Ain't nothin' good south of the river." He looks at me—hard. His stupid eyes now filled with fear.

Something about Badger being straight scared like this makes my shiver come back. But I'll deny that if anyone asks.

Chapter Five
Digits

Historical Record

Date: Tuesday, 26 June 2068.

Location: Lander's End. Fellowship, established 2030, post-Darkening.

Population: Approximately 265. Minus 4 in approximately seven hours.

Mission: Book retrieval.

Intended Target: The Last Bookstore.

Distance to Target: Unknown.

Team: Gideon "Digits" Rylace, age 11 (reporting). Logan Rylace, age 14. Mateo Johnson, age 13. Jack Weller, age 14, team leader.

Objective: Retrieve medical journals pertaining to current anticoagulant disease and ailments.

Affliction: "The Bleeds." Current survival rate: 0%.

Defenses: Wrist shooters (4) and ammunition. (Unstable) explosive devices (from unstable source).

Additional Supplies: Limited food and water.

Approximate value: 2 days.

Potential Threats: Animal threat, probable (threat scale: 3-5). Environmental threat (threat scale: 2-4). Underfolk, no reliable intel (threat scale: 7-9). Blighters (threat scale: immeasurable).

Personal observations and assessment: If I am intended to die young, let it be known that I died nobly. In defense of my community and my brothers by blood and by heart.

Chapter Six
Willa

Time is running out.

Willa paces in the darkened shed, sweat dripping down her back and fogging her safety goggles. She's been working on this particular formula for five hours straight, pausing only to calculate mixtures and restart the homemade swamp cooler that keeps her specimens cool. She loves her husband, but when it comes to mechanics and solar powering them, Garrett is more theory than practical application.

Still, the mixtures remain stable.

Her dark hair, once one of her favorite luxuries, is now streaked with gray. Too soon at only thirty-three, she thinks. That's about as much time as she can donate to vanity these days.

Her people are dying and she is their only living hope. Her dearest friend may be next. The likelihood of Avery's death is a percentage too terrifying to even consider.

When the EMP changed their world some fifty years ago, three things quickly became hot commodities: guns, money, and medicine. Guns that—to hear her mother tell it when she was still alive—were way too important in what used to be the United States. The gun stores, police stations, and army bases were looted within forty-eight hours of the EMP—because, in times of fear and doubt... kill it.

Soon enough, these hostiles realized that ammunition would run out, and they were lost. Manufacturing without significant power wasn't an option, and their priorities were wholly out of whack. They were among the first to go.

The next commodities were paper money and gold. Another futile endeavor because they instantly became useless fodder, so barter replaced money. Nevertheless, people robbed, killed, and died for it. They too were quick to go.

Finally, third on the New World's Most Wanted List: medicine. Specifically, pharmaceuticals. Her mother had talked of the insane prices and processes in the development of "modern medicine." A concept at which Willa could only shake her head. Before, they had access to all manner of supplies, resources, and power, and yet greedy corporations wasted so much time on legislation, lobbying, and profit that they lost the thread: to save lives.

The irony was that post-Darkening, people hoarded these life-saving medicines, profiteering for their own selfish needs. Self over community. And the bitter truth was that any "modern medicine" eventually expired, and these merchants, profiteers, and hoarders were quick to die out as well.

And then there was nothing.

Except her people. Her grandmother had been a nurse in a large hospital. Her mother, a PhD and pediatrician after her. Until the Darkening—then her mother became a scientist, a pharmacist, a medicine woman of the New World. She passed her knowledge on to her daughter. The botanicals, the homemade, the Earth-supplied. Some worked. Others didn't. Her mother had followed the same medical texts that Willa now pores over obsessively, their pages frayed and dogeared, all in an attempt to help. To heal. To fight.

Sweating and cursing in her makeshift lab in front of a row of beakers, Willa has tried to mimic these drugs. To cook, blend, dry, mix, reshape, and reconfigure into some semblance of the miracle treatments they used to be. But the world is a crafty foe sometimes. The illnesses have evolved while the medicinals she's blended have not. Old diseases returned: rickets, polio, botulism, tetanus—all results of a world plunged into darkness and fear, and a race incapable of adapting in time.

New World diseases were born.

Skin rot, dysenteric epilepsy, and the Bleeds—the mother of all medical nightmares, where people's bodies just begin to revolt from the inside. Organs shut down, arteries collapse, and one's own blood betrays them, becoming poison in their veins. Willa's on her second year of trying to fight this beast and the losses are piling up. She spends most of her days trying new mixtures, doubling down on old ones, and watching them repeatedly fail.

She is losing. The method of transmission is unknown, so there's no known means of prevention. No protection. Sometimes its victims go slowly, taking several months. Sometimes, mercifully, it's faster—weeks or days.

Two weeks ago, Avery began presenting symptoms. Whether out of love or stubbornness, Willa had refused to label it. Her son, Mateo, was born in Avery's home, and Avery was the second soul he laid eyes on. (This was only because Garrett, all six and a half feet of him, had passed out cold.) Avery's children, Jack and Beckett, might as well have been her own. They were siblings to Mateo. Garrett and Reese were best friends as well. Willa's life, its very foundation, was slowly being torn out from under her, bruise by bruise on her "sister's" body.

Willa wipes the sweat from her brow and tries again, adjusting her mixtures.

She will not go down without a fight.

Xander

A set of doors bursts open and a screaming figure stumbles out into a darkened passageway, cradling a hand to his chest and leaving a pool of blood in his wake. He is filthy, bleeding, and terrified. Firelight shines behind him and a massive body hurtles out of the doorway after him. It is so large and wide that it nearly blocks the light. In the doorway, watching the pursuit, a shadowy man steps forward, holding a torch and humming "Merzy Dotes" as the broken figure runs.

The tune and humming distort. It is eerie, low, and disturbing. The shadowy figure, his trench coat outlined in the doorframe, seems to vibrate with excitement. He bends down and wipes a spot of blood off his boots. Firelight glints off their exposed-steel toes, showing the laces strung with human teeth. After wiping off the blood, the gloved hand picks up something nearby on the ground.

Three human fingers.

The humming stops and is replaced by a low chuckle. In the distance, a final scream erupts, followed by a savage, inhuman yell of triumph and need.

The chase has ended. The prey ensnared.

Chapter Seven
Jack

The figure is there.

It's right behind me. I can't see a face and I try to run, but no matter how fast I will my feet to go, I am barely moving. RUN.RUN.RUN. It reaches out for me. There's a HUMMING, a song. I don't recognize it. I'm yanked back. I fall backwards and stare up. The hood leans over me and I smell blood. I look to where the face should be—

"Jack."

"NO!" I bolt upright, ready to run, fight, anything.

I'm in my bed. I wipe the sweat off my face and try to slow down my heart. It's beating too fast.

"Jack." I squint at the figure in the doorway. Disoriented. It's Mom. Just Mom. *Breathe…* It was just a dream. The same dream. *Breathe…* She walks past Beckett's bed and sits down next to me. "Are you okay?"

I nod.

She wipes hair from my forehead. I let her because I'm just so glad it's her. Her hand seems small—delicate. "Nightmare?"

"I guess," I say, and then I'm quiet. I don't want to talk about it. Somehow, she knows this. My mom and I sometimes have this silent talk. Like, she can understand what I'm saying without my having to say it. So she just looks at me. There's a peace to her in spite of the dark circles I pretend aren't there. She smells like…

her. Dried thyme and woodsmoke with a little flowery something under it all, jasmine maybe.

"Okay." She makes like she's going to stand and winces, trying not to let me see it hurts.

"Mom?" I don't want to see her hurt. "Can you just… stay here for a minute?" Part of me is asking because I just don't want to see her struggle, but the other part? The part that I don't want to talk about just wants her here. Brushing my hair. Being my mom, keeping dark things away.

"Sure." Her eyes are a little glassy. "Do you want to talk? You know, about…"

"No." I really don't. She looks at me and nods. I lie back down and move over. She lies down next to me and we look up at the rafters. Beckett hung all these paper and tin star mobiles there when she was seven, even though I told her they were on my side and I hated them. Now, I'm kind of used to them. Maybe I even like them. Mom and I lie there and watch them gently twist and sway.

It's our thing. Sometimes we don't talk at all. Sometimes we talk about everything. Sometimes we laugh so hard we wake Beckett up. Which isn't pretty, let me tell you. Now, it's just us. Being here, under the tin-paper sky. Mom takes my hand and begins massaging it. She's done this with us since we were babies. My hands, Beckett's earlobes.

It's about the greatest feeling on Earth.

As she kneads my hand, she sings, low and soft: *"Great big house in New Orleans… Forty stories hi-igh. And every room that I've been in, filled with chicken pie."*

35

Mom tells us that her people used to live in New Orleans. I've seen an old photo-picture, torn and faded, of my great-grandmother in front of her house there. I guess it's all under water now. Forgotten. The song is ours, though. And it works—my eyes start to drift closed.

It's a "moment." My mom talks about them. Those points where you are super aware of yourself, your life, everything all at once. I try not to think about what is coming. What needs to happen. What I need to do. I just want to live in this one small moment and sleep with her voice in my head and her smell all around.

I know Becks is awake in the next bed, listening. I hope she is living this moment too.

Because what's coming… It's bad.

Chapter Eight
Beckett

There is only so much I can take.

I think if I laid out ALL the crimes, ALL the torture, ALL the tricks and jabs and downright EVIL that Jack has committed against ME, I'm pretty sure EVERYONE would understand why exactly I have to WHOMP him.

See, this morning I rode to school with Dad. I usually ride Oliver—that's my bike, and oh, WE WILL GET TO THAT in a minute. Dad and I have been fixing up Oliver for the past month. Huge new tires, padded seat, ape-hanger handlebars—whatever that is. My dad says they came from a motorcycle called Herman Davidson, which made me laugh out loud—giving a motorbike a human name. It's not like it's a bike or something. Anyway, Oliver is about to look even cooler than before. And before? It was hands down the coolest moto-bike in Lander's End.

So I ride to school with Dad on Mercy, his stallion, who is the fastest animal on four legs I've ever known. Dad says I can ride him solo when I'm thirteen. I get to school and I see Jack and his dumb crew hanging out in front, waiting for Miss Eunice to ring her bell. I go in cause I have to find the homework that I had to turn in on the Great War of 2025 that led to the Darkening. So the bell is rung and the kids file in like normal. There're about thirty or so of us, from ages ten to sixteen. The young ones go to the primary school in the back church. So I'm talking to Nava, getting my circuit board ready for engineering, when I glance around.

NO JACK.

No Logan. No Mateo. No Digits. And THAT'S what triggers my alarm. If Digits could LIVE in school, he would. He soaks up learning like dust soaks up rain.

I get a weird feeling. And I KNOW this is not just a regular ditch day.

And I know where they are going. NATCH! I grab the sides of my desk so I don't just stand and run out screaming after them. I know I can't draw attention or Miss Eunice will tell my folks. So I sit there and grip my desk until my knuckles are all white and I'm starting to see spots in front of my eyes—for TWENTY-TWO MINUTES.

I thought I was gonna die. Finally, Miss Eunice releases us for a "ya-ya break"—that's where we get to go outside and run around, have snacks, play, and get our ya-ya's out. I am first out the door. My ya-ya's are gonna come out all right. Gonna come out all OVER Jack when I catch him. My farm is one and a quarter miles from the school. I run it faster than I've ever run. Anger is great fuel, I guess. When I get close, I make sure Mercy is still gone and check if my mom is outside. She isn't. I sneak around to the barn. If I'm gonna catch them, I'll need a faster way. And then I open the door and MURDER becomes a good idea.

Oliver is GONE.

All I want to do is scream. Scream so loud and long that my vocal cords burst. But I can't. I have to get moving. I sneak into the back of the house. I know exactly which floorboards are noisy and which are safe. Mom will probably be sleeping in her room. She gets tired so easy these days. I sneak up to my room and pack up some supplies. On the way back down, I grab some more from the kitchen. I get to the back door and run for the shed. That's where Jack parks his stupid bike. Of course, the motor has been broken for about two months. He could fix it, but he doesn't really mind pedaling everywhere. Ew. If it were a broken BOOK, I bet he'd be all concerned but… it's just a bike. A janky, slow pedal bike.

Oh, Oliver…

I put on my pack and break for the tree line. I know the back path, along the road. It's a shortcut through town to the Wall—but more importantly, my dad won't see me if he heads home. I pedal so fast my legs burn. I know exactly where they are headed.

Since Lander's End was founded, we've had the Wall. Even then, the townsfolk knew how important it was to keep Blighters, Underfolk, and anyone with ill intentions out. We get wanderers every now and then. We will let them in—or the sentries and board members do—if they seem peaceful. Only a few have ever stayed. It's been so long since the Darkening that anyone left wandering is usually only fit for that. They don't take to "town life." They end up moving on. So the Wall is as high as the highest redwood. Because that's what it's built from. The gates themselves are trunks, bolted together with iron and steel and reinforced on both sides. They can be opened by two to three grownups. You can't climb the Wall because it's covered in pig fat every week to make it too slippery, and it has spikes along the top except for at the sentry stands.

So that leaves only one place where Jack and his busted band of goochers could have gone.

The Rabbit Hole.

It's a hole that someone dug under the Wall a long time ago. It's on the outer south edge, so not many patrols pass. Many of the kids know about it, but it's never come out to the grownups. Lots of kids, including Jack and I, have gone to look at it. It's covered by a big boulder that someone rolled there after the last Blighter scare.

Would take two grownups to move that... OR three goochers and Mateo.

Chapter Nine
Mateo

"Donkey turds, you guys! How much longer?"

i already wanna pass out. From up in front, Jack says, "3 minutes less than the last time you asked."

Oh—an' of course, blowhard Logan's gotta chime in. "We've been walking 4 like 12 minutes, Mats. Brace up."

"You brace up. i'm the 1 walking behind a backpack fulla bombs! It's stressing me out." See, somehow, after we crawled through the Rabbit Hole, i ended up walking behind Logan an' his stupid pack loaded full of Badger's explosives. BADGER. I mean, he's near simple on a good day. No telling when those bombs are gonna go off.

Donkey turds.

Digits signs something 2 me. His hands are moving 2 fast. So as usual, i look at Jack. He tells me, "Dige says, 'Burping stresses you out.'"

Does not. i gulp a buncha air an' let out a monster BURP. Prizewinner. 'Cept after, i always gag an' stuff. The guys start laughing an' trying their best burps. Logan's always tryin' 2 beat everyone… always. Dang, if that guy weren't so wily, i'd lay him out an'—

Jack holds up a hand 2 stop. We're quiet 4 what seems like 20 minutes an' then this frazzled ol' coyote slinks past. We see lotsa them around Lander's End, but they're all shifty an' scared. We just run 'em off. This one doesn't seem 2 scared. It stops an' looks at us. All creepy-like. We all go quiet an' still, everyone watching each other.

Suddenly, Logan bursts out, "GIT! GO! GO ON, NOW, BITCH!"

She just runs away, real fast. Dang! That was CLUTCH. "Yeah, bitch! Ha!" i add. Now Digits is shakin' his head at me. "What?" But i don't really wanna know cause—yep—there they are—his fingers goin' all fast.

i can't be bothered 2 try an' read them, so i just sign, "Okay, i get it."

Suddenly, everyone's crackin' up. Crap. Logan, still laughin', says, "You just told him you love your toilet."

They bust up again, an' i can't help myself. "Well, I do. Gonna be a janky nightmare having 2 wipe with a leaf out here." i'm laughing—but 4 real, what if i grab some sumac? Have 2 ask Jack be4 i reach—he an' Beckett know all that stuff. His mom is really in2 weeds, plants, an' all that. Helps my mom with her potions an' cures.

Donkey turds.

Just started thinking about moms. i look around, trying 2 change my subject. It's nothing but forest an' trees an' bushes an' trees an' dirt an'... trees. i mean, at first i was excited 2 be PAST THE WALL. None of us have ever been. Sure, we talk about it sometimes, but now that it's happening, i'm just hungry. i had 2 come, tho. i mean, it was my idea. i can't invent it then expect Jack 2 go alone. Plus, then Logan would have claim 2 it. Natch that. Also, i'm tired of people dying an' my mom being so... heartsick over it. i could save the whole town with this plan.

Then, outta nowhere, Digits points at something.
i look.

2 late.

He punches my arm an' signs, "KNOCK." See,
THAT one, i know. Knock is where you point at
something and if the other person looks, you get 2 punch
'em in the arm. i dunno who started it or where it came
from—i just know that we've always been playing it.
Digits always dominates. But i keep trying. i let a teeny
bit of time pass, tap his shoulder, point, an' punch his
arm. "KNOCK!" i holler. Digits is shaking his head an'
crazy signing at me. Oooo—he's bent up. He gives up
an' just acts out that he DID NOT LOOK. i saw his eyes
shift, tho… i think.

"You looked. i knocked. i win." Digits just gives
me a look an' keeps walking.

We walk MORE. Jack an' Logan are talking low
an' serious. Sometimes i get, like, jealous of their talks.
Sometimes i wonder if i'll get 2 talk like that with one of
them… or anyone. But 4 right now, Digits is a way
easier target. i give him a flat tire, steppin' on his shoe.
He punches my arm. i punch his an' BURP in his face
then gag right away. He starts laughing. There's
something kinda… magic about Digits's laugh. It makes
you think good things. i love this about that little guy. i
love it so much i TACKLE him.

It's ON! We're wrestling all over the dirt an' then
Jack an' Logan are there an' it's a good ol' dogpile. HA!
i RULE at dogpiles—i can pin all of them.

Right now, everything is just like home.
Donkey turds.
That just made me think about moms.

Chapter Ten
Logan

It's starting to get dark.

We've been walking for a long time, and of course, Mateo thinks he's gonna die. Typical Mats. Sometimes… that guy. Badger's "map" is all crazy, but Jack seems to be moving pretty confidently. I guess if anyone could make it out, it would be Jack. Or Dige.

I wanna say stuff to Jack. I want to tell him it'll be okay, but I don't want it to be all weird. He's got that look. I mean, he knows I've got his back. Crawling under the Wall and risking our lives with a pack full of explosives says that, but still…

"Hey, Jack?"

"Yeah?" He's looking at the map. Not me. Good.

"It'll work. Ya know, the books, the medicine. We'll get it, and it'll work."

He says nothing. Keeps walking. Digits and Mateo are messing around a ways behind. Up here, it suddenly feels way too quiet. Oh, natch, I blew it.

"Thanks." He glances back at me and nods. It's fine. Enough of that.

Later: Girl talk. Always happens. I ask Mateo about his options. "Well, if you had to kiss one of them, who would it be?"

"If I HAD to? Well… I guess Bailey. She's got clutch hair."

Jack pipes in. "Seriously, Mats? 'Clutch hair?'"

"What?! I dunno. Look, we can't all have like FIFTY girlfriends like Logan."

I smile and Digits signs to him, "More."

I don't have fifty girlfriends. Maybe two. Or three.

"How many have you kissed?" Jack's acting all swick, like he doesn't wanna know, but I know he does.

"A few." I shrug. Gonna make him work for it.

Of course, Mateo chimes in. "Ohhh! How was it? Wet? What if you burp?"

I bring it back to Jack. "You've kissed someone, right?"

He won't look at me. "Not really," he mumbles.

Is he walking faster? "Well, Teelah likes you. You should kiss her."

And Mateo is off again. "Jackie and Teelah, she wants to get a feel-ah! Wheel-ah, deal-ah, peel-ah—BOOBS!"

We start laughing because... well, Mateo does that. Suddenly Jack stops, hard. "SSSHHHH!" We all go real still, listening. I don't hear anything. Digits just watches me. We're all quiet. Waiting.

Except Mateo is never good at waiting. "I don't hear—"

"Listen," Jack says and looks around. We all do.

"Jack, there's nothing," I whisper.

"Exactly. No sounds. No wind, no critters... no birds." We listen more. Suddenly, it's even quieter. And then...

Mateo farts.

Of course, we start laughing. "What? I get nervous," he says, smiling.

Even Jack is smiling. "Dang, Mats—what did you eat?!" He waves the air in front of him.

Then ALL HELL BREAKS LOOSE. There's a huge crashing sound. Something is ramming through the brush toward us!

"RUN!" Jack yells.

I'm fastest but I'm behind Jack AND I'm carrying the explosives. DO. NOT. THINK. ABOUT. THE. EXPLOSIVES. So I just run right on his heels. I wanna push him faster but I know he'll fall, plus I have to keep Digits on my right, keep my eye on him. He <u>falls</u>. But before I can even turn to grab him, Mateo sweeps him up and we're running again. We're crashing and running forward, and that sound—branches cracking, bushes being ripped up, loud breathing getting closer. Jack dives over a huge fallen tree and disappears. I dive right behind him. Digits and Mateo do the same, landing on me. I hold in my yell—Mateo is heavy—and scramble around to look out. Digits and Mateo untangle and peek out beside us.

The only sound is our breathing.

I don't see anything. Without taking his eyes off the forest, Jack pulls out his slingshot and loads a rock. Smart. I do the same. Digits does as well. We each cover a section in front of us. Except Mateo, who's tearing his pack apart looking for his slingshot.

After a few seconds, I lean toward Jack. "Elk?"

He shakes his head. "Not this low."

"Cougar?"

He shrugs, still watching. "Pretty rare. Plus, I don't think it would have stopped chasing us…"

Mateo leans in—he can't whisper for crap. "Is it maybe out there, like, hunting us?" He lets out a tiny fart but this time no one laughs. We just breathe and watch.

Well, Dige plugs his nose and grimaces, but he was right next to him so… We wait.

There's nothing.

It seems like a long time. Mateo is all caught up in searching his pack, so he can't interrupt and—

There. Something is making its way outta the bush. We aim. Except for Mateo.

It's a stupid coyote.

We all breathe, and I even let out a little laugh. None of us care two wicks about the stupid things. Though this one does look a lot scrappier than I've seen. I start to stand up to shoo the ugly thing away and—

Another one comes out. And another one. And one more.

Four in all.

They step out and stand in a kind of half circle. Staring at us. Low growling deep in their throats. They all look mean and hungry. Jack turns and starts getting all his ammo out and spreading it on the ground. For rapid loading and firing. I do the same.

"Okay," Jack whispers. "Nobody panic—"

Mateo is scrambling all around in his pack and pockets. "You don't panic! I can't find my—"

NATCH. Two MORE creep outta the bush. The last one is probably the biggest I've ever seen. The whole pack starts growling louder. They take a couple steps toward us. The teeth. Sharp and jagged. Digits hands Mats a bunch of his green ammo. We load up and aim. They seem to have stopped moving, but their growling gets louder. One barks and I can't help but jump a little.

"Well, what the hell do we—" Mateo whines, but then they suddenly break for us ALL AT ONCE. I think I hear Jack scream, "FIRE, FIRE, FIRE!" I half stand behind the log and rip off one rock after another. I see Digits and Jack out of the corner of my eye doing the same, and same with Mateo—but let's be honest, he might as well be aiming at the sky, he's such a crap shot. I land most of my shots and hear a buncha yelps. I can see them getting hurt. Jack lands a couple great ones, and all but three of them peel off and run yowling back into the forest. I'm getting ready to feel good, but I see that these three—including that gigantic one right up front— are still coming. We start firing with all we have, but the shots either don't land or the coyotes just don't care.

Mateo starts screaming, "Throw bombs, Logan! Throw the BOMBS!"

"THERE'S NO TIME! SHOOT!"

We double up our rocks and two of them peel off, yelping and running fast the other way, but that one big bastard... Just. Keeps. Coming. I'm reaching for my ammo but I'm almost out. He's so close—there's spit and foam and blood in his fangs—he is so fast—it isn't gonna work. I grab for Digits, to cover him and wait for the worst, as HE LEAPS—

And something hits him right in the eye.

Whatever it was, it flipped that giant piece of crap RIGHT OVER in MIDAIR. He lets loose with this huge YELP and lands on his back.

He hits with a WHOMP but quickly shakes it off and scrambles back to his feet and lets out a long wail. Where the eye was is just a bloody socket. Gross. Gross AND screw you. He looks at us outta the one good eye, lets out another whine, and turns and trots off into the forest. We watch him go for as long as we can see him. And even after we can't, we still stand there. Watching.

"Pretty sure I just crapped my pants," Mateo says, which breaks us outta being frozen.

We all take a bunch of big breaths. I let go of Digits, checking to see if he's okay. He nods.

"Nice tap, Jack." And I mean it.

He looks at me, shaking his head. "Boss, wasn't me. I was out. Digits?"

We both look at Dige, who shakes his head and climbs over the log. He searches the ground and comes up with a big bloody yellow stone.

No. Friggin'. Way.

We all look at Mateo, who looks just as shocked as we are. "Wait, no, you guys. I don't have any—"

"AMMO?" We all jump at the voice and spin around. "Well, that's cause you suck at war, butt munch."

And there, grinning, with a big pack, a slingshot, and a huge bag of ammo… is Beckett.

Chapter Eleven
Digits

Beckett.

Standing there. Like fire in a dark sky. I don't know about romantic love, but I can imagine it would feel something like this. My whole chest swells with pride at just knowing her. But no amount of real surprise. I knew she'd track us. I smile to myself—but Jack is angry. It's the same anger Logan feels toward me when I jump the bike over Gullen's Ravine.

Fear.

And under that: love. But in the moment, when you're the subject of that mix, you can't focus on its source. Just the anger. It's complicated. My hands don't have the words to explain it to them—it would take too long. So... we walk again. It's getting darker. That seems fitting.

Situation Report: Quiet.
Status: Fractured, but alive.

Chapter Twelve
Reese

The cistern is leaking and the water gears aren't moving smoothly. There are leaves and debris on the sun panels and the fence needs mending. The horses aren't turned out and the council wants a late meeting about the Wall Patrol. These thoughts run through Reese's mind as he works underneath the tiller, which has begun to rust. He sweats. He toils. He torques the wrench until his muscles shake.

And none of it can fix her.

The wrench tears free and cuts his arm, leaving an angry bloody gash. He lies there under the tiller, heaving air and trying not to break.

They met when Avery was seven and he was nine and her parents had come to Lander's in the last big migration. Before that, Lander's End had just been forming as a township. Its governing board was newly established and Reese's father was its first lead councilor. The population had swelled and they saw the need for a set of laws, boundaries, and working order to go along with their new numbers. The council soured some, who moved on to other areas, but it solidified those who stayed. It was still spitting distance from the Darkening, and these were the formative years. Lander's benefited from its organization and thrived. With the fall of the southern states to floods and famine, the last big wave of migrants drifted west. The heartiest of these travelers made it to Lander's End.

Avery was among them, along with her mother, father, and baby sister.

He first laid eyes on her when her family was negotiating a plot of land with his father. She was inside an old camper shell, which had been drawn by a set of horses. Avery peeked her head out and, spying the nearby horse trough, jumped down, raced toward it, and plunged her head inside. She came up soaking wet with a "whoop!" and a grin.

And Reese would swear to this day that he felt his heart explode.

Two kids, a farm, a life, and countless memories later, he lies on the floor of their barn, willing that same muscle not to stop from grief.

He watches the blood from his arm pool and drip to the dirt floor.

"Reese? You in here?" Garrett—his neighbor, best friend, and closest thing to a brother—stands over him.

Reese inhales sharply and shimmies out from under the tiller, willing his voice to remain steady. "A-yuh, right here."

"Have the kids come here?"

"What? No… uhhh…" Reese checks his watch. Late—much too late for them to be gone. How long has he been trying to busy himself away from feeling?

"Mateo didn't come back from school. When I went by, Miss Eunice said none of them had been in class."

"Wait—who's 'none of them'? Cause I know Jack and Becks went to—"

"None of them, Reese. As in Jack, Logan, Gideon, and Mateo. She said Beckett was in First Hour but then disappeared after that."

Reese inhales. "Well, they're probably at the pond, then, or in the field. Did you—"

"I rode everywhere, asked everyone I saw. No one's seen them."

All of Reese's rambling thoughts are suddenly slammed aside by one: *My KIDS.*

He brushes off his hands and ties a rag around his cut. "Where's Willa?" he asks as they cross outside to the paddock.

"She went to check over by East Road."

"Can you get her and have her come stay with Avery? I'm going to the Wall." Reese grabs his saddle off the gate and trots over to his horse.

Garrett splits off left toward his own mount, already in line with the plan. It's how they always work. Garrett knows him almost as well as Avery does.

Don't think about her.

Just bring her babies home.

Xander

A lone man enters a battered city ravaged by war, time, and abuse.

Crumbling buildings, broken windows, trash, and decay prevail. Any remaining survivors exist through pain and treachery alone. No hope lives here. The man walks toward a barricade, a makeshift wall of rotted-out vehicles and ancient appliances piled atop each other to protect the city's inhabitants: the Blighters.

A few men carrying primitive weapons patrol its border. They are covered in sores and mutter to themselves. They visibly tick and shake uncontrollably. The result of "Kuru"—a disease brought on by cannibalism, a common practice amongst them.

No one ever gets in, unless allowed, and very few ever go out.

The man stops. He is unnaturally tall and wears a roadworker's vest, yellowed with age. He nods to the sentry, who motions for him to pass through an opening between a steel railcar and an eight-wheeler truck. The vested man belongs, so he may enter without sacrifice. He climbs deftly through the wreckage and enters the city.

This is Blighter territory. Filthy men, women, and children skittishly move about. Most are covered in lesions and festering sores, their despair leaking to the surface. The giggling, muttering chatter of the insane is a constant soundtrack of these forgotten as they aimlessly wander, waiting for their next order. As the man walks purposefully to the only intact building, they part en masse. He takes no notice, his focus solely on the rotating door of the once-majestic hotel, which he pushes open with ease.

The building, a place where dignitaries and presidents once supped and slept, is now a broken husk of its former pride. The wallpaper frayed and peeling, its carpets torn and its furniture butchered. A few transients huddle against the walls, keeping to themselves. Murmuring and... waiting.

The vested man approaches a large wooden door and knocks. It creaks open as a small bald albino stands aside to let him into the enormous ballroom. He is Shadow, second-in-command of this broken kingdom. He motions for the vested man to step further into the cavernous room, before returning to his own work.

The vested man surveys the giant room. Two walls are lined with hundreds of old gas cans and a few relic generators. Along another wall are countless bottles, barrels, and containers of water. The last wall differs from the others. It is nearly antiseptic. Its cabinets scrubbed and filled with pristine coolers and containers of all sizes. Shadow is filling one of them with bags of collected blood. He pulls out a bag and holds it up to the light, examining it before cataloging something in an old notebook.

"Hello, Eugene." A gravelly baritone voice rings out from across the space, distracting the vested man, who immediately stands straighter. He timidly approaches the far end of the room, where a huge chair faces a fireplace. He waits.

A gloved hand appears at the side of the chair, beckoning him forward. Eugene approaches and steels himself for its inhabitant. The chair turns, revealing the

King of the Blighters. Xander is deceptively handsome—
somewhere between his fortieth and fiftieth year, with
black-pupiled eyes that seem to swallow light. He wears
a trench coat and one of his sleeves is rolled up,
exposing a bruised arm. Next to him is an IV stand with
a blood bag currently draining into his vein.

Xander smiles widely. "And what news do you
have for me today?"

Eugene clears his throat, speaking slowly and
carefully. "There's no word back from the two scavenge
crews. Word at City Barricade is that some got too sick
and others ran off."

Xander's eye twitches with frustration, but he
quickly recovers. In his free hand, he fondles a swatch of
old, worn material. It is flowered and frayed. It looks as
if it belonged to a baby blanket from a forgotten time.
Xander rubs it rhythmically, gaining calm from the
motion. "Well, that's... troubling. Who gave this
'word'?"

"Um... a border guard." Eugene's confidence is
quickly draining from his body.

"Hmmmm, so no names on these guards?"
Xander waits. Patience is his specialty.

"Didn't catch any names. But Lowside Crew is
heading in with a couple Clean Bags they think might be
workable."

"Shadow will determine that." They both look
over at the small man, who COUGHS once then nods in
response before returning to his blood cataloging.
"Well, Eugene, that—that is very good news. Any idea if
the new vessels are diseased?"

Eugene shakes his head. He is starting to fidget. Nervous.

"Any sores? Chattering? Coughing?"

"Uhhh, they look okay. A family. Refugees. They look good." Eugene waits, unsure.

"And what of the census?" Xander gently removes the needle and caps it, swabbing and patching his arm. He looks at Eugene's blank face and speaks more slowly, pointedly, as if to a child. "THE. HEAD. COUNT. Where might we be?"

"Say about three hunnert."

"Hundred," Xander corrects.

"Yep. That."

Xander stands and walks toward Eugene. "Tell me. Is that more or fewer than last month?"

Eugene's eyes are looking everywhere except for Xander's face. He wants to bolt, but there is nowhere for him to go. Finally, he answers, "Fewer."

"How many fewer?"

"'Bout a hunnert—hundred."

Xander paces around Eugene, quick, graceful, and lethal. Eugene's eyes are downcast as Xander's rapid-fire questions continue. "Do you know where that 'hunnert' went?"

"Naw."

"Are you sure?" Xander gets closer.

"Uhhh."

"Think," Xander presses.

"Can't figure. Maybe the sickness. Maybe the bends."

Xander puts his gloved hand on Eugene's shoulder. "Perhaps if your lot stopped eating human *flesh, you wouldn't go insane, right? So the 'bends,' as you call it, might just be survival of the fittest, yes?"*

Eugene is hopeful. He tries for a joke. A forced camaraderie. His only goal is to leave the room alive. "Like, they ate folks then went a-babbling up into no man's land or down with the Underfolk. Idjits."

Xander chuckles. Charmed. Eugene looks relieved.

"And what of HER? Any news?" Xander's black eyes belie a desperation he cannot cap, in spite of his lethal smile. His hand never leaves Eugene's shoulder.

Eugene slowly shakes his head.

Xander now stands closer, just behind him. Deadly. Soft-spoken. "Remember when I told you she was rumored to be hiding with the Unders? That you should look there? Tell me, did you?"

Eugene again shakes his head. "Uhhh... them tunnels, they're too dark an'... twisty. But I got you people—clean people—some water. Can't do nothin' 'bout that hunnert—"

Xander LAUGHS hard at this. Eugene, suspicious, tries to smile. Still laughing, Xander pockets the fabric swatch, walks up behind him, and gently puts a gloved hand on his shoulder. Xander laughs harder and Eugene finally starts to relax and GIGGLE along.

Without hesitation, Xander SNAPS his neck. Eugene crumples to the floor. Xander shakes his head, disgusted. "It's 'hundred.'" He turns to Shadow, his heart rate never spiking. "Remove that. Find her."

Chapter Thirteen
Jack

Sometimes Mom says, "I'm so angry, I could spit fire!"

I get it. Beckett is one of the only people who makes me that angry. It's so big sometimes, I get a bitter taste in my mouth. But also, it makes me so… sad inside, I guess. It's complicated. I would say that I can't believe she followed us, but that wouldn't be right. I absolutely can. No matter how hard I tried to prevent her from coming, she still came… and there's nothing I can do about it. No. I don't want her here. I considered turning everyone back, but we can't. She knows this. There's nothing I can do, so no matter how mad I am, we call a truce. But I'm not happy about it. If anything happens to her… Well, I can't think about that right now. I tried to protect her, and I failed. So right now, I'm so angry I could spit fire.

I can forgive her, but I can't look at her. I force myself to keep walking, head down and focused on our destination. I'm lost in all the thoughts of what to do, when I hear it: water. A lot of it. We clear a stand of trees and I see it. The river. We knew we'd have to cross but… *Natch.*

"It's swollen from the last rain," I say, trying not to sound small.

We walk a little farther and look up and down the banks, searching. Not too far away, we find a huge oak that spans the water. A. Perfect. Bridge.

But it's old-looking… Not very comforting. Not at all. Maybe not so "perfect."

I see Digits just slump down to the dirt, staring at it. Beckett sits next to him and they start signing. Of course, Mateo can't track it. "What's he griping about?"

"Mats, you learned to sign a hundred years ago with the rest of us—how come you keep asking me?" I say, searching the banks.

Mateo whines, "His fingers are all fast. All of you—with the super fast fingers…"

I'm about to start arguing with him, cause I have a huge, wet, bigger issue on my mind, when Logan interprets. "He can't swim."

I hadn't even thought of THAT. I'm an idiot. Mateo, of course, decides to argue. "Can too! Dige, I've seen you—at Wilson Pond. I was right next to ya—"

Beckett chimes in. "That's, like, four feet deep, dingleberry. He can touch there. THIS"—she motions to the raging river. "Little different."

"You're a dingleberry," he mumbles.

"Wow, good one, Mats," she fights back. But then Digits is signing really fast to Beckett—and of course, Mateo is lost again.

"You guys?! Little help?" he whines, pointing at Digits and Becks.

I turn and see what they're saying. I "read" for Mats. "He's saying, 'You can't always carry me. There's a time for everyone to stand. This is my time. This mission is bigger than each of us and all of us.'"

Mateo interrupts, "Well, what the hell is that—"

Now Beckett speaks as she's signing to him. "He's saying this is about securing our future."

"Natch, I know that—my mom—" Mateo tries, but now all of us are standing around Beckett and Digits.

Digits signs faster, getting worked up. Logan reads, signs, and says, "No, Mats. Not just us. Not just Lander's End…" And Digits just repeats a sign. Three fingers of each hand revolve around each other. Again. He looks at each of us as he does it. There's a moment, then Logan turns to Mats. "Not just Lander's End. He's talking about… the world. About saving the world. Humankind."

We just stand there. A moment, inside a moment. I feel like someone kicked me in the guts, it's so big. I think for the rest of my life I'll be able to see Digits, sitting beside his worst fear, making the sign for "the world" over and over.

"Whoa." Typical Mateo. But it breaks the… *depth* of it.

Beckett stands and helps Digits up then… hugs him. I can only think *whoa* when I see Digits's whole… soul respond to that hug. Stunned and exhilarated, he hugs back. Fiercely.

Whoa.

Pretty sure he'd stay there until he died, so I try and move this along. "Look—the tree will hold us okay. We just have to go slow and make sure it's not rotted. There's no going back."

Beckett removes herself from Digits's embrace, crosses to the tree, and starts kicking at the roots. Digits still holds his arms out, trance-like, as if she's still there. It'd be funny if it weren't so… true.

Logan gently puts Digits's arms down as he passes. Everyone joins in, congregating at the tree's base. We all test the strength of it, the base, the roots, and then we start piling nearby mud around the bottom, stabilizing it. Beckett is next to me. I'm trying to drown out the sound of the water, which is so loud it sounds like it's screaming… at me. "How'd you get outta school anyway?" I half shout to her over the deafening water.

"When I saw that ALL of you guys were gone, I ducked out before Second Hour," she says, already wrist-deep in mud.

Of course, Logan is there with the challenge. "Well, how'd you catch up? I mean, Jack took—"

I glare at him, which Beckett immediately catches. "Jack took my BIKE? Yeah, I saw that. Well, when I cut through town, I happened to see MY bike behind Badger's. So I rescued it."

Logan can't leave it alone, dammit. "He didn't see you?"

Beckett just looks at him. They do this a lot. Like two roosters in a barnyard challenge. Finally, he shuts up—for now anyway. After a few more seconds of all of us digging and patting and grunting, Beckett glances at me. "What'd you trade him for?"

No sense trying to hide anything now. "Info at first, some directions. He gave us an old bookmark. But Digits found the actual map."

"And BOMBS! Whole pack fulla bombs!" Mateo chimes in. How the hell did he get mud on his forehead?

Beckett is staring at me. She finally nods. "Not bad."

Whoa. "Seriously? I thought you'd lose your mind?"

She starts digging again. "You're doing whatever you have to. I'm here to do the same."

I can't help myself. It's just so... I smile at her. I'm proud, sure. But I've also known her our whole lives. "That, plus now you can get me back when I least expect it, right?"

She looks up at me and grins with her muddy Beckett grin. Fine. So long as we understand each other. Yes, it's a "moment."

One by one, we stand back and consider the tree bridge. We've done all we can with mud to stabilize it on this end. Underneath the screaming water, it grows quiet. I'm sure they're all thinking that this is where we pass the "point of no return." I get a body chill. This is suddenly too real. I was so busy thinking about my mom and Beckett, I never considered that I would be putting all my friends' lives at risk. I know I told them it was their choice. Hell, I asked all of them about a thousand times to THINK about what they were doing. I want to tell them to go back. I'm about to open my mouth and let all this brain firing spill out when—

"Fine, I'll go first." Damn her stubborn self. Before I can stop her, she's up on the end of the log.

"Becks, wait!" I reach for her but she sticks her stupid tongue out at me and steps out onto the trunk. She bounces gently then harder, testing its strength.

No one breathes or moves. When the tree doesn't instantly plunge into the angry water, she grins and walks across. Just. Walks. Right. Across. Like it was a stroll across a summer porch.

Damn Beckett. I admire her as she jumps to the opposite shore.

"Uhhh, Jack?" It's Logan. I'm about to ask what the hell he wants when I look down.

I'm standing in the center of the dang tree, midway across. Right over the biggest, fastest river I've ever seen. Guess my body followed Beckett right out into terror. So I decide to trust it. I look up at Becks again. Her face is janky. Like she's half-scared, half-confused. I understand that she doesn't quite get what the hell my body is doing either.

Play it smooth, Jack. I wink at her and step out carefully, one foot in front of the other. I am near blind with fear, but I can't let them see this. Especially Becks. I get to the other side and jump down like some kinda outlaw. "Come on—" I start to call to them, but my voice CRACKS. I clear my throat, playing it off, but I can just FEEL Beckett smiling at me. "It's stable." Little better. Do. Not. Look. At. Becks.

Logan approaches the log and I see him signing to Digits, "You want me to go in front of you or behind you?"

Digits signs back, "You first. Then me. It's okay. I'm okay." Jeez, that kid has grit. Logan looks at Mateo, who nods in return. Logan knows he'll get Digits's back. And just like that, Logan is across, standing next to me. I would hate him for his ability, but this wasn't his usual showboating. He raced across so he could coach and guide Digits.

He, Beckett, and I all crowd around the opposite end of the log to help draw Digits's focus and cheer him on. "Slow and steady. Just don't look down. Look at me," Logan signs to him. Digits does as he's told and steps out, cautious but steady, staring at Logan. It's going well. One foot in front of the other, Logan signing, "You got it," "Easy," and "Good" the whole way. Mateo is close on his heels, within grabbing distance. They're focused. Steady. As they reach the halfway point—

CREEEEEEAK.

The tree slowly shifts, ever so slightly, but that sound—that sound speaks of more to come. Digits's eyes flash white and wide. The tree shifts a few inches further and he drops to his belly and hugs the trunk for all he's worth.

Mateo shouts from behind him. "NO, DIGE, just—awww, boss! Logan, tell him to KEEP GOING!!"

Logan jumps onto the end of the log.

"No! You'll shift it more!" I yell at him, and he instantly jumps back down. The water looks bigger, angrier. Logan steps to the side and frantically signs, "KEEP GOING!" to Digits, who inches forward on his belly. The tree GROANS in protest.

Mateo is looking at us, trying to stay steady as it shifts another couple inches. "You GUYS?" Now Digits is inching wildly on his belly. It's crazy-looking but the guy is actually making progress. He's so close. Ten feet maybe. Mateo is almost on top of him, making a pushing motion with his hands. Just then, the tree shifts again, this time almost a quarter turn. Digits's hands and feet scrabble for a hold, but as it turns he can't counter-crawl fast enough.

He slips sideways on the log.

Beckett screams.

Mateo dives.

He actually DIVES through the air like a flying squirrel, GRABS Digits's knapsack, and TOSSES him to the shoreline, just out of the water. Digits lands hard but intact and dry from the knees up. Mateo struggles to stay upright on the log, but his momentum is too much. He does another humanly impossible leap, this time toward shore. He lands face- and belly-first in the rocky sand, next to Digits. We hear all the air leaving his body.

"AAAAHHHH—I BROKE MY PENIS!!!" He rolls over, clutching his parts.

Digits tries to cover his laugh. Logan and Beckett help him up and I cross to Mateo. "HOLY CRAP, Mats! You THREW him!" I say, not wanting to touch him quite yet.

Logan chimes in. "That was BIG CLUTCH, boss! How'd you even—"

Mateo smiles and slowly raises one hand, wiggling his fingers. "Fast fingers, boss. Fffffaaaaasssssttt fingers."

Chapter Fourteen
Beckett

I'm scared.

So the river was big, sure, and it was pretty spooky watching Digits almost go in, but THIS? This is all KINDS of janky. We're standing just beyond the river at some old water outlet that goes right into a mountain, and Jack is doing his "Jack thing," where he gets all moody and paces. He keeps staring at it, then at the map, then back at the tunnel entrance and crinkling his brow.

So, yeah. I'm scared.

But I can't let any of these goochers see it cause then it will just give them more reason to judge me as "too young" or "like a girl" or... "that Beckett." 'Cept Digits. He's NEVER been that way, thank you very much. The thing is, here's where I need Jack to go ahead and plunge on in so I can "draft" off his courage. My dad taught me that drafting is where you get right behind someone—on a moto-bike works best—and you ride in the pocket of least resistance. Riding off their power, letting them cut the wind.

Jack finally says, "Listen, you guys, you can still go back—"

Logan chimes right in. "No way, boss." Like he's not next to me, swallowing so hard I can hear him.

Mateo blurts, "Seriously? You said 'no going back' at the river. How many times you wanna dare us?" I think he's as nervous as the rest of us, and it comes out a little harsh. Bad timing.

Jack spins on him. "This isn't a joke! I told you I could do this on my own! Mats, I mean, why are you even here?"

See, I know that when Jack feels scared or threatened, his first reaction is swift and severe, but Mateo... He's, ya know, Mateo. I see hurt right away in his eyes.

"Cause—cause I can help with stuff, ya know. Cause... Digits can't save the world alone! Also, I KNOW what's going on, okay! My mom's been all over Lander's and the outer towns, and people keep dying, an' every time she loses someone, she cries—an' doesn't sleep, and gets sadder and sadder, and they JUST. KEEP. DYING. Sooner or later, she's gonna get it. THEN WHAT, Jack?!? Huh?! You don't always know everything, Jack!"

He's sweating and all red in the face. He stomps over to a huge rock, picks it up, and just HURLS it off into the trees. Then just stands there, huffing and puffing, staring at Jack.

Damn, Mats. Nice one. I grin at him and so does Digits. Logan just stands there, probably wondering if he can throw that rock farther, dang goocher. Jack just looks right back. Then gives a small nod. Crazy how a movement so small can say so much. Mateo nods back, and without a word, they both start walking to the pipe.

And just like that, I'm drafting.

The tunnel is small and smells old. There's water at the bottom, but not too much. We all walk single file, stooped over. It's pitch black almost right away. Jack and Logan pull out their torchlights and shine them, but even so, it only shows more blackness up ahead.

68

Drafting. I'm walking behind Jack and I want to hold his hand, but he's got the map and his torch, and I can't be girly, so I reach behind me in the gloom and grab Digits's hand. I make it seem like it's for safety, like I'm looking out for him, but I'm just scared and wanna hold on to someone I know.

It helps a lot. Digits gives me a nod, all serious, and it's so... sweet on him that I just smile back. Yeah, it helps, and I don't care who thinks I'm girly. I AM a girl for natch's sake.

"Looks like this bends up ahead then starts to go down," Jack says.

"That where the Underfolk live?" Mateo pipes up from the end. DANG, MATS, REALLY?!

"I dunno, Mats. I just know this is the only way into the city without going through Blighters," Jack calls back.

"You think the Underfolk really eat people, Jack?" Mateo blurts.

I can hear Jack's teeth gritting. "I dunno, Mats."
Don't keep talking, Mats. Don't. Don't. I am willing him not to talk, but he keeps going.

"Well, has anyone ever—" We all turn on him.

"Shut up, Mats!" Logan.

"NATCH'S SAKE!" Jack.

"Don't." Now I'm willing him out loud.

And Digits just stares at him and makes the "lock it up" motion at his own mouth.

Jack sighs and tries to end it. "Look, Mats, it's just a myth, okay? A legend that people have passed down and built on, designed to scare kids."

"Well, it's working. Also? They're gonna go for me first, ya know," Mateo declares. "I'm juicy."

See, this is where Mateo is at his most valuable. He can make you grin when it's the last thing your face wants to do.

"Yeah, but you also butt-blast when you're nervous—so, built-in security," Jack replies. Clutch, Jack. Total clutch. We giggle a little, but then Mateo actually lets out a tiny, scared fart and we all bust up. It's one of those kinda uncontrollable laughs, like when you're in school or overtired. It keeps building.

Through his giggles, Mateo continues, "Shut up, you guys. Farts are probably like a—a dinner bell to them."

And we all lose it. I'm bent over, trying to walk and catch my breath. Logan is hiccupping and Mateo is farting. Jack keeps fighting to control himself, which makes it all the funnier, and Digits, well, his giggle... It's perfect.

Suddenly, Jack freezes, hand up. "SHHHHH! You guys, shut up!"

Mateo ducks. Logan, Dige, and I grab and load our slingshots. I'm looking everywhere, trying to find my target. I just hear our breathing.

There is nothing. Then Mateo whispers loudly, "Logan! Get the bombs!"

"What?! No!" Logan whispers back.

"Oh, fine. Easy for you—they won't eat you. You're all bones and anger."

We go still again. Listening. Aiming. Nothing. For a quick second, I think I see a shadow way up ahead that looks darker than the others.

Did it just move?

It looks like a person. I'm crazy, right? I blink. Hold my breath. Count to ten. It just stays there. No movement. It melts into the same color as the rest of the shadows. BRACE. UP. BECKETT.

Jack exhales and lowers his slingshot. I lower my slingshot. Jack checks the map. "I think it's fine. We gotta keep moving."

Mateo is still spooked. "We could stop and eat, make sure it's all—"

Jack glares at him. "No. We gotta keep going. There's a fork a ways up, may widen out."

Everything in me wants to turn around, but I know we have to keep going. I know that Jack feels the same. If we wait too long without moving, we just may never move. I pocket my slingshot, ready to follow, but then stupid Logan chimes in. "But we don't even know—"

That's IT. I turn and give Logan my special stare. "Jack's right. We keep going."

Logan stares back at me from behind Digits. Digits is just looking at me. A tiny smile. Helps me hold the stare. Logan finally shrugs, like the plonker he is, and we start walking again. As we do, Jack glances back at me. He gives me a little smile and a nod.

Guess he can draft too.

Chapter Fifteen
Mateo

Every step we take gets us closer 2 being eaten.

i feel like none of them even understand this cuz they just. Keep. Moving. 4ward. i am hearing things the whole time. Like, i'm sure we're bein' watched. i bet it's an Underfolk just drooling and waiting 4 us 2 hit a trap. Then… dinnertime. i don't say anything, tho, cuz it's bad enough they're already scared, an' i don't wanna be the plonker that makes it worse.

Finally, we hit a fork in the tunnel and Jack stops. He stands an' looks at his janky map 4 like 20 minutes, so 4get askin'. i'm gonna sit and eat something, dang it, cuz if i'm gonna get eaten, i'm going out with a full belly. i reach in2 Jack's pack that he set down. i know he's got the good jerky his mom smokes. Lots of it. He won't miss some. Dige sits next 2 me and grabs an apple from his pack. Logan comes over and Digits hands him some food. We're all usin' up our torchlights, like batteries don't mean a thing. i don't care. i want all the light i can get right now.

i keep lookin' in2 the dark, an' i swear someone's lookin' back. Makes the meat go sour in my stomach. Natch. Jack an' Beckett are arguing over the map. Surprise.

"Well, what does it say?" Beckett asks him in that tone she gets.

"It says, 'Go left, right here!' I was just stopping 2 take in the view," Jack spouts back—he's got his own tone.

Beckett keeps looking at the map, staring real hard, and says, "We should go right." Like she knows. Plonky girls.

"And how did you come up with that? Other than that it's the opposite of anything I said?" Jack's gettin' riled up. i would tell him 2 take a rest an' have some jerky, but i just finished all of his.

i'm staring in2 the dark, waiting 4 some Underfolk 2 come running in, an' suddenly Logan also perks his head up, listening.

"I just have a feeling," Beckett tells Jack, an' i can see they have no idea of the shadows or whatever it is that Logan is hearing. i try an' listen real hard. i don't hear it but i see Digits watching Logan's eyes. Makes my belly clench again. Logan gets up real slow, like he's trying not 2 make a sound. Digits an' i get up 2, but i have no idea why.

"Guys?" Logan whispers.

"Oh? Really?" Jack says, oblivious. "Cause I have a feeling 2. I'm feeling like you should shut up." Jack's gettin' louder at Becks. Doesn't even hear Logan.

Brace up, brace up, brace up…

"Guys," Logan whispers at them a little louder, looking all around.

i start 2 hear something. Sounds like… scratching. Skittery and spooky. Oh, NATCH—i betcha them Underfolk all have busted ol' long nails and are crawlin' along toward—

Beckett is almost yellin' now. "You always think you're the BOSS! Just cause you're older—"

"GUYS!" Logan finally shouts. Yes, good. Let's go! Logan shakes the back of Jack's shoulder, handing him his pack, an' points down the tunnel. Jack finally stops an' looks. He an' Becks both crouch, ready, cause now we're all hearing the Underfolk's nails and they're comin' RIGHT THIS WAY. Everyone takes out their slingshots. Loaded. Ready. I wait, shakin' an' prayin' that i don't just pee my pants or faint or scream an' never stop.

It's a PLONKY RAT.

1 stupid rat comes scrabbling outta the dark. It's ugly, sure, and kind of giant, but i almost wanna pick it up an' kiss it cause it's not a cannibal with long nails an' a hungry temper. It stops a ways from us in the fork an' just looks around, all stupid. i breathe out like i've been holdin' my breath 4 days.

"Ha! That was YOUR pick. See, I told you—" Beckett starts, but she doesn't finish. Jack shushes her real loud an' then we all hear it. That scraping an' scratching comin' from the same direction, but it sounds... BIG. We're all frozen, waiting. The scratching gets louder an' louder, like it's inside my head, an' then suddenly a GIANT, janky, WORLD of RATS comes pouring outta the same tunnel the 1st one came from.

Only they're just... wrong. They're all white. No fur. Red eyes, an' twice the size of that 1st rat. Every part of me freezes up as they all attack that 1st rat an' tear it 2 shreds. The screeching and tearing makes me wanna be as deaf as Digits. i might be screaming 2 but i can't tell. The wave of monster ghost rats is now coming STRAIGHT 4 US!

Jack breaks my freeze by yellin', "RUN! 2 the RIGHT! GO! GO!"

And we are all flyin' in2 the other tunnel. i wanna scream an' cry, but i gotta make sure Digits is okay. Logan's pullin' him by the hand so i gotta watch his back. Means i'm backend again, but i don't mind that as much as front. The whole bunch of ghost rats just streams right past us in2 the left tunnel like a white river. i keep runnin', following Jack in2 more dark. i'm just happy they're behind us.

We are still runnin' and i glance behind me toward where we were. i squint real quick cause i could swear i see fire glowing back there… an' the shadow of a person…

Just run. Brace up an' run.

Chapter Sixteen
Logan

Dang! I hate running behind people.

I mean, I know Jack's gotta lead cause he has the map, and he's gotta keep Becks close, but I'm third and that just… burns me. It's like waiting to get let outta school but time slows down. Never knew two people could be so slow. I've also gotta hold Digits's hand, which makes running all out harder. He's fast, though. Just glad to be away from those… whatever they were. Like creatures that used to be rats. Never thought rats could get uglier. I was wrong. I can hear Mats start wheezing in the back. He'll pass out before he leaves Digits uncovered, though. I look up ahead and can see the tunnel opening up into a bigger space—maybe we can—

And we're DOWN.

Jack trips on his way into this part of the tunnel. Beckett flies right over him, and then we're all one big mass, groaning and grunting and trying to breathe.

I wouldn't have tripped. That's all I'm saying.

Jack is up, reaching down. "Becks, you okay?"

Beckett is squirming all over. "Yeah, but I got someone's FOOT in my PRIVATE SPACE." I take account of my feet. Not me. We squirm and struggle. I'm trying to get Digits up. Mateo finally stands—think he was the one mucking it all up anyway, and he—

WHOOSH!

I'M FLYING. There are screams and yells and my stomach drops out like when I jump the bike off Galway's Hill, but not in a fun way. We're trapped ten feet off the ground in a huge net. I think it's got all of us, but the plonker thing is swaying and twisting, so I can't tell for sure. Can't tell whose arms and legs belong to who cause we're all tangled.

"WHOSE HAND IS THAT?" Becks yells.

"Becks, stop moving, you're only making it worse." Jack. Good.

"IT'S THE CANNIBALS, THEY'RE GONNA EAT ME!!!" So I know Mateo's up here, but I gotta focus.

"MATEO, SHUT UP!" I feel Digits find my hand and sign "OKAY" into my palm, so we're all here. I'm spinning and can't get loose, but we're all together and that's good. Wait—is that a PERSON down there? I see firelight—NATCH THIS—

"SILENCE!!" the figure yells, interrupting my concentration.

It's wearing a big ol' cape thing with a hood. Underfolk. A hand reaches up from the cape and stops the net from spinning and swaying. Good thing too, cause I know Mats was gonna puke on it if we didn't stop spinning. We kinda untangle but not much. Everyone's everything is touching and twisted in everyone else's everything.

Mateo is whining like a new puppy. "This is it, man, this is it, we're all gonna get eaten! Me mostly, but then you—" he whispers in a yelling kinda way.

"Shut it, Mats!" Jack real-whispers.

Becks is twisting something crazy trying to see the figure. "Uhhh, hello? We mean you no harm. We just need to pass through." Jack is glaring at her and shakes his head. Warning her off. Like THAT'S ever worked. She keeps going. "We didn't mean to trespass or—"

"I. Said. SILENCE!"

Beckett lets out a tiny yelp as the figure steps forward and circles under the net. None of us can see under that hood. Dang. I hope it has a face. I can feel Digits start shaking as he just keeps signing, "Okay? Okay? Okay?" into my hand. He can't see my face so he doesn't know how to read the situation. In this case, I think that might be good.

I sign back, "OKAY." Even though all I wanna do is cry.

Digits can only see Mateo's face, dang it, and of course, Mateo can't hold his mud. "Look, sir, I know I probably seem meaty to you, but I'm just big boned. I promise, I probably taste like horse crap—"

"SHUT YOUR MOUTH!" the figure hollers real loud.

The yell janked us all out, but also… it sounded like a… woman. I try to replay the voice in my head, but I can't concentrate cause of Mateo's tiny whimpering and the loud, slow CREAKING from the net as it swings real slow.

"I think you all made a mistake… And this one was a BAD one." Yep. That. Is. A. Woman. Still might not have a face, though.

Beckett leaks a couple of tears and looks at Jack. Once, I would have made fun of her for this, but seeing her now makes my throat get all thick. Jack stares back at her and puts a finger to his lips. I wish I could see Digits's face. I sign, "OKAY" again—and try to believe it. He's looking around crazy-like, trying to find…

something. Suddenly, I just get… FURIOUS. NATCH this robed lady for making Digits shake, Beckett cry, and—ohhh—I wanna scream at her. I wanna grab her by her janky, no-face neck and twist.

"You have trespassed on HALLOWED GROUND." She paces below us. "Your penalty… is death. A SACRIFICE. You will be CON—"

"Oh, JESUS, Mel—they're ready to stroke out. Will you stop it, already?"

It's ANOTHER voice. Can't twist to see, though. Everyone's looking around trying. I'm frantically trying to sign, "Someone else!" into Digits's hand when another person in a hood walks over to the yelling one and smacks her on the back of the head.

All playful. Like one of us would do to another.

"Dammit, Blue, one of them was just about to pee his pants," the yeller says, but all normal now. Definitely a woman.

"Nuh-uh!" Mateo blurts.

Great, Mats. The second figure steps closer and pulls back its hood, and it's got a face. It's a woman. Just an ordinary-looking woman. I actually think she looks… nice. But… old. I mean, we don't see a lot of older folks in Lander's. Usually, like fifties is about the tops. Lotta disease and… oldness takes folks out. This woman has silver hair and bright—crazy bright—blue eyes. Like they see extra far. Not at all like the Underfolk from my nightmare. The yeller lowers her hood, kinda huffy-like, and she ALSO has a face. She's a woman but her hair is cut super close, like a guy. She's older too and looks like she could eat a person or two without thinking twice.

Blue holds up her torch and steps closer. Her eyes lock on Beckett.

She smiles. Not an "I can't wait to eat you" smile either. It's… beautiful, really. Beckett grins right back. Maybe this is some plonky, weird "lady language," cause I have no idea what the hell is happening. But Digits isn't shaking anymore and my chest loosens—a little.

Blue says, "I'm Blue. Hi." Real kind. Beckett says it back, quiet-like but just as warm. And they just grin at each other.

NATCH THIS. "Excuse me, ma'am, but if you guys aren't gonna eat Mateo here, then could you maybe let us down?" I bust out. Blue nods at the shorthaired one, who pulls out a really big knife and begins to cut us down.

Janky lady language.

Chapter Seventeen
Digits

It's slow motion and hyper speed all at once.

We are running, then falling, then flying. Then trapped. I cannot see who begins and ends where. So, I feel. I feel the breathing. Fast and terror-filled. All of us. Like one organism. There is vibration. I know who is talking but not what they say. I only see Mateo's mouth. I am trying to find her face. It's unreachable. I reach for Logan's hand.

"OKAY," I tell him with my fingers in his palm. I reach my other hand to find her back. Touch. It's all I can do. I try and read through her breathing. So fast. She's afraid. I apply pressure, trying to soothe.

I watch Mats's eyes. They are wild. They go wider. I follow his gaze. A person. Underfolk? Mateo yelling about them.

Her breathing is in gasps. She's speaking—it vibrates. Not yelling. She flinches. Screams?

FURY. I want to destroy the figure that harms her. My body shakes with it. My hand repeats to Logan, "Okay? Okay? Okay?" Is she okay???

He signs back, "Okay."

I twist to see. The figure is pacing. I cannot see its mouth to read. I feel Beckett hitch. Crying? No. No. No. I twist to see. I catch another figure emerging.

A woman. Richer in years. Impressive. Is this the face of cannibalism?

I feel Beckett's back relax. She is calming. I send more pressure. Is it what quiets her?

The other figure removes her hood. Old as well.

The blue-eyed one stares up. Beckett speaks. Short. She breathes easy. If she is safe… I am as well. We are being cut down.

Come what may. I am okay… Okay. Okay.

Situation Report: Captured.

Status: Cautious, but hopeful.

Chapter Eighteen
Garrett

Since the children went missing, Garrett has been turning over all the survival tips he taught Mateo. Skinning food, trapping animals, basic defense, and what greenery you can and can't eat. He knows Mateo has retained precious little because, well, he's his mother's son and leads with all of his heart and none of his head.

Still, the lists replay. A background mantra to help him from spinning out of control.

They're all hanging by a precious-thin strand and he knows that if one of them snaps, they will all tumble straight into sheer terror and grief.

Garrett paces the small space of Avery's kitchen. Nearby, Reese is talking into the ham radio, letting Benton and the men know that he and Garrett will soon be crossing past the Wall. He's telling them in no uncertain terms that this is not a matter up for discussion.

Earlier, they got word that the kids were seen talking to that janky half-wit Badger. So Garrett and Reese paid Badger a visit and had a "talk" with him. It didn't take long for Badger to tell them what he knew and to re-create the map that the kids were following to the city.

Hell on Earth. Disease, famine, Unders, and... Blighters.

Garrett looks across the kitchen at Willa, who stares back hollowly. He knows the wear on her runs deep. He sees it in her eyes. He hears her when she cries at night in her lab. He watches her travel from deathbed to deathbed, trying nobly to rail against the ravages of this disease. He hears her mumble, near delirious with exhaustion, about the need for information, the need for more books, the mixtures, the text, the rules… As if there are any rules to apply to these times.

Now their babies… gone.

His baby.

He loads his rifle with homemade buckshot. Reese ends the transmission and looks at him. They've grown up together. They are brothers, despite their skin shade and blood. To the death, they will fight.

They will follow their kids into hell.

They will bring their babies home.

Xander

"Please. Let me go. Please." The woman is terrified. Dirty. A wanderer. She is no more than twenty, but her skin looks clean.

Xander looks up from his desk. A behemoth of a man effortlessly holds the squirming woman. *"Silence her."*

Without missing a beat, the large Blighter presses her carotid artery and she passes out. He lays her on a table as Shadow rolls over an old medical irrigation stand with several IV bags. Shadow sticks the young woman with a needle, skillfully hitting the vein on the first try. He withdraws the needle and inserts the IV tubing into the open hub.

The bag slowly fills with blood. Shadow inspects the sample under a microscope.

"Is it clean?" Xander is hopeful but masks his desperation with nonchalance.

Shadow looks at the girl and tilts his head: clean enough. Two blood bags are now filled.

Even unconscious, the woman looks faint. Xander walks over and cursorily inspects her. But something stops him. Something is wrong. Too familiar. He leans over and smells her hair. Almost feral.

"Is it her?" the large man asks hopefully.

"No, but she is close." Xander pulls out the flowered blanket swatch from his pocket and inhales deeply. *"Ash, prepare the search party."*

The large man nods and leaves. The only sound in the room is the woman's labored breath.

Xander climbs onto a table beside the young woman and the IV stand. He rolls up his sleeve, revealing broken veins, abscesses, and bruises. He motions toward the prone woman. "Drain it."

Shadow emits a cough then finds a vein. The transfusion begins.

As he watches the life drain out of his latest sacrifice, Xander remembers _her_. At first, she was just an experiment—a lifeline. But she became something more. She made him feel. And even though that weakened him further, it allowed him some hope in this graveyard of disease and decay. He inhales again, willing her scent into his lungs. She has never been this close before. He can feel her. And he will find her.

--

"They are ready for you."

His third-in-command has reappeared at the door. Ash is Xander's protector, a perfect physical specimen despite his slow mind and his eyes, which are completely black. Xander pulls down his sleeve and gets off the table, barely glancing at the ripe corpse beside him. Not all donors are completely drained; some are allowed to survive. It depends on their quality... and his mood.

The Blighters in the hallway cower as he passes. Some bow. They all avert their eyes. He has succeeded in making them both dependent and terrified.

Xander enters the crisp night air, followed by Ash and Shadow. Several dozen Blighters with torches approach from all directions, their dots of firelight converging around a huge pile of rubble. Xander looks on as they "gear up," arming themselves with all *manner of medieval-looking weaponry. Shadow winces as he pulls on protective clothing. Ash dresses Xander in protective body armor. It is an intricate process.*

Xander's mind is heavy. "The issue, Shadow, is that ours is not a sustainable system. Our food is nearly gone, there is nothing of value left to trade, and... this." Xander points at a huge pile of corpses. A few Blighters in vests throw more on the pile or burn them in a giant pit. "Our 'army'? Dead or dying. At this rate we will have nothing to take over the North—or anywhere for that matter. I need to think bigger. A way to gain... influence. Tonight, we will take care of the Underground, though it's but a drop in the bucket. Your transfusions are... adequate, but we cannot save anyone from a tainted well, nor can we arrest the plague. We need to think larger. I need you to find a cure, Shadow. SHE is the beginning of that—her blood has revived me from the brink time and time again. From her, you will concoct that cure. With that, I could rule... everything and all people. What wouldn't you give for life itself?"

Shadow stops as Xander stares at him. He shakes his head, fear contorting his otherwise blank features. He opens his mouth and emits a moan. He has no tongue.

"Shadow, you know what happens when you argue, yes?"

Shadow goes silent, his place in the chain long ago established through a thousand cuts, blows, and tortures.

Just behind them, completely hidden by another collapsed building that has fallen against it: a glimpse of the NORTH STAR SYMBOL peeking out from the rubble.

The same one from the BOOKMARK the boys had. Its significance lost in the firelight and building rage.

Xander stands on top of a pile of rubble as Ash stands guard. Shadow crosses his arms, surveying the crowd. Every now and then, he stifles an errant cough. Below them, the Blighters are gathered, trembling with need and anticipation.

"Hello, kith and kin. You have your assignment. Apparently, the other crews found this task too difficult. They couldn't fulfill their duty. They did not have the tenacity to find what I seek. They were daunted by selfish needs. They. Were. Weak."

He scans the crowd, working them like a hypnotist. Stoking their fury, slowly building it. "So I've gathered a select few. My BRAVEST. My STRONGEST. My MOST TENACIOUS, UNDAUNTED WARRIORS." A CHEER goes up, unintelligible in its need. They would kill anyone for him, including themselves. His eyes glisten with insanity and power. "That's you, brothers and sisters. I know you will find what I seek. I know you will not tire, you will not weaken, and you will not give up. We start with the Underground, and we do not stop until SHE is found and returned—unharmed. Any others are yours to… do whatever you wish to."

The crowd goes WILD, surging and swelling like one giant organism.

Xander reaches into his bag, removes the flowered fabric, and hands it to Ash, who inhales its scent deeply, turns wordlessly, and descends through the frenzied crowd. They follow him, still yelling and cheering.

Xander watches for a beat as Shadow erupts in an involuntary coughing fit. Xander looks at him, fear and anger in his eyes. "I have plans, Shadow. Don't jeopardize them."
He steps down, following the raging horde. Shadow quickly follows, tears streaming from his eyes.

Chapter Nineteen
Jack

For the life of me, I cannot read these women.

Whenever we tamed a new foal at the farm, Dad would always tell me to try and "read" the animal. Watch his eyes. Feel its muscles. I watched him do it. I learned. I eventually tamed our last three foals. I got so good at reading them, I could anticipate their movements. Their moods. Their tempers.

These women seem kind. The one woman's eyes—clear sapphire blue, so bright it's hard to look at them—are kind eyes. She has an easy smile and a gentle tone. I don't even try to read the other one. She's hard, but she jokes easily with Blue. But they are Underfolk. They supposedly EAT people, and we are following them down a dark tunnel to our possible death. I wish my dad were here. I wish it so hard my teeth grit.

As I'm trying to figure out a way to break us out of this, Beckett chimes in. "But you're Underfolk, right? I mean, the ones people talk about?"

Man, I could throttle her.

Blue glances back at her—they seem to like each other already. *What the natch?*   "That's right. We're Underfolk. My name's Blue, and that surly gal back there is Mel."

"Do you eat people?" Becks blurts.

I guess we were all thinking it. Her way is just a little more… direct. I try to jump in, cause… well, a part of me doesn't actually want the wrong answer just yet. "Becks! Of course they don't. I mean… you don't, right?"

She looks back at me, and I can see her bright blue eyes. They're dancing. Mocking me. Is she playing with me? I mean, her mouth has a little twist, like my mom gets when she's joking with me, but she DOESN'T ANSWER. I can't take this. "WELL?! Are you folks cannibals or what?!" I shout, looking for some kind of exit. I can feel all of us holding our breath.

She bursts out laughing. I'd be mad if it weren't such a thick, friendly sound. Cannibals can't have joy like this, right?

"Course not, son. That's a silly tale. One that we don't try to discourage, though. Keeps people—outside people—from getting too curious about us."

We stop and my whole body tenses. I hope that laugh wasn't a lie. I want to grab Becks's hand, but I have to keep mine free in case I have to fight. The tunnel has widened and we're standing in front of a MASSIVE steel door. It's been welded and reinforced. It's about the strongest-looking door I've ever seen, but you wouldn't see it unless you were looking. It's real craftwork.

Cannibals or not, these folks know how to use a torch and hammer.

Blue bangs hard on the door three times. We hear chains and cogs working on the other side. It's slowly pushed to the side with a groan and two women stand there. They're dressed like Blue and the other lady, and they don't seem to have kid bones sticking out of their mouths.

A good sign.

"Hey, Jamis, Dolly—these are some guests. Try not to eat them, okay?" Blue jokes.

Again. Ha ha. I hear Beckett gasp. She's staring into the space beyond the door. Everyone is staring, that same busted look on all their faces. Then I turn and see what they're seeing. It's huge. Imagine if someone put an entire town in one grand space and enclosed it. As we stumble in, I see that one whole wall is greenery. Hanging herb gardens from ceiling to floor. My mom would lose her mind! There are stalls set up as a kind of marketplace, trading animal furs, fruit, vegetables, cookery, tools—even one with wooden toys. The back wall has large doorways leading further underground. I can see into a huge kitchen area with stoves and refrigeration bins, pipes and columns leading up through the ceiling. The center is set up as a communal meeting place with picnic tables, chairs, a small stage, and a firepit. They've rigged electricity, generators, and lighting.

I can hardly breathe.

There are people everywhere, all of them dressed in similar faded, draped clothing. They all seem friendly and happy. They take notice of us—but not like we're the main course. I feel my shoulders start to relax a little as a tiny goat trots right up to Digits and starts nibbling at his pants. A curly-haired boy in a striped shirt, about my age, runs up and tries to pull him off. I smile at him, trying to be all friendly. He grabs the goat and just stares at me. It's a weird look. I can't place it, but "welcoming" wouldn't come right to mind. Before I can talk to him, I'm pushed forward with the group. I lose him in the shuffle.

"You guys sure have a lot of old people," Beckett comments. I swear! The second it hits her janky brain, it's out of her wonky mouth.

"BECKS!" I reprimand. Even if they aren't cannibals, it doesn't hurt to be polite.

But Blue smiles at her, her eyes crinkling just so. "I imagine we 'old people' are kinda scarce elsewhere. We have a longer life expectancy down here." She starts to lead us through the common area as she talks. "We have our own water, pumped in through refashioned tunnels from the river up top and purified. Our power is sun given, and we have battery and generator backups, but those get hinky sometimes."

Some of the smaller kids are now following us, peeking out and giggling. I make a goochy face at one of them and he laughs out loud.

"Everyone has a job here, and folks start training young," Blue continues. "We have some great cooks, our own agriculture, even livestock. We're independent. That's how we get so 'old,' and that's also why we don't advertise. We have no war with anyone, but we also know good from bad kinds." She has led us down a long, large hallway, lined with door after door. She stops in front of a set of double doors. "This is a locker room with hot running water for showers, if y'all wanna clean up."

Beckett motions down the hall. "What are all the other doors for?"

"Those are our dwellings. Enough for a small family in each. We've built out steadily for over forty years, and we'll keep going. Gotta keep up with the population."

At that point, an old guy—maybe fifty, maybe more—in specs and a green woolen sweater walks up. He smiles at us, all warm, and puts an arm around Blue's waist. She smiles back. They are obviously… you know. Together.

"This scrappy, not-quite-as-old fella is mine. You can call him Gentry."

He grins at us again, not like he wants to barbecue us, and nods. "Hello, young wanderers." He lowers his voice a touch. "Seems like you bagged a full load, Mama. Any sign of HER?"

Blue just shakes her head. "Not sighted, but there were plenty of signs. You know how she is."

He nods, rubs her back. "Sure enough. She'll straggle in when she gets hungry."

What's all this natch about, then? I'm about to ask when Blue pulls out a key, unlocks one of the doors, and opens it. She holds out her hand, motioning us inside. Not an oven. Just a room—bunkbeds and blankets. It'll sleep six. Comfy enough, just not home.

"Why don't y'all get some shut-eye. In the morning we can get y'all cleaned up and fed, and then we can talk about what brought you this way and what you're needing, okay?" Blue says.

Of course, Becks blabs. "We're going to the Last Bookstore to get a book that'll save my mom's life. You guys ever fight the Blighters? Do you ever go outside? You ever see the sun?" So much for keeping things on the down low. Damn Becks.

Logan speaks my mind for me. "Damn, Becks, take a breath."

Blue just grins at her. That crinkly-eyed, charmed smile. "I got nothin' but answers for you, little thing. In the morning, after you clean up."

I try and steer my way out before Becks can blurt anything else. "That means you're ripe, Becks."

True as a sunrise, she spins on me. "Yeah? Well, I can wash, but you'll always be ugly."

Mateo laughs. "Ooooo, natch, Jack—she gotcha, Stinky!"

They barrel into the room and all four of them are jumping on beds, claiming them and roughhousing. Blue smiles at us and slowly closes the door.

I wait a couple of seconds, listening at the door, then try the handle. Locked.

This could be just what it seems, some friendlies on the way…

Or we could be dinner.

Chapter Twenty
Beckett

The Underfolk's world is AMAZING.

I mean, they've got their own gardens with the biggest fresh vegetables and fruit I've ever seen. My mom would lose her mind! There are kids and people all over the place, and they all seem very friendly. They have easy smiles like Willa—like, no matter what is going on, good or bad, she stays calm.

And then there's Blue.

I mean, I know Jack wants to protect me, but I had a sense about her the second I laid eyes on her. She's NOT gonna eat us, I'll tell you that. She's strong and seems… wise, I guess. Maybe because she's old. Don't see many old folks these days. She reminds me of Mom, the way she looks at me. Like she just knows what's going on in my head.

After we divvy up the bunks—I get a top one, thank you very much—we all pretty much fall right asleep.

In the morning, the guys let me shower first so I can have the room to myself, which I think is pretty nice since they can generate some janky STINK! I know we fight sometimes, but I also know they love me. Like family just does. So we all take the good with the natch and carry on.

After my shower, I wander around the main area. There's so much to see and smell, it really is like another world. Outside the showers are these other big doors. One of them says "NURSERY," and I just imagine all these sweet babies lined up in cribs. I reach out to open the door—maybe I could hold one—

A hand grabs my shoulder and I jump.

It's Blue. She's looking at me with that knowing smile. Can't help but smile back when someone does that. I learned this from Mom. Just might as well grin back, even if you look like a plonky kid.

"All cleaned up, I see. Feel better?" She smiles.

"That shower was excellent. All the soaps smelled so good—I almost ate one." It's true. I stayed in there a lot longer than needed, just sniffing on all the soap.

"Where are your troops?" Blue looks around.

"Ahh, still in there. They let me go first for privacy. But they're also filthy—like, always—so extra time under water will be good for them." And if they come out smelling like that soap, all the better.

Blue leads me away from the nursery doors. "Bet you're hungry."

DAMN RIGHT. I nod at her. Looking at all this swank food has my stomach all loud and grumbly. The smells too. Like, I wanna just swim in it. Blue leads me to a table nearby and we sit across from each other. A lady comes by, wearing the same stuff that Blue, Mel, and now we are wearing. It's soft and smells of that wonderful soap. I feel like one of them. Like I belong here. The lady puts down some plates, napkins, and spoons, and leaves. I start to feel my mouth water just thinking about what she might bring. I hope I don't start drooling. THAT would be about as busted as it gets.

"How old are you, Miss Beckett?" Blue asks.

"Twelve and a half. You?"

"Sixty-three… and a half." She smiles. "Whereabouts are you all from?"

"Lander's End. It's out through the drain at the river and through the Dark Wood," I say, feeling kinda proud of us.

"Well, that's a mighty long journey. You all must be made of fortified stuff."

I duck my head a little cause of the blushing, but there's a smile there too.

The lady comes back with two big bowls of stew and a whole plate of shiny, perfectly cut-up fresh vegetables and places them down for us. I thank her and she smiles. Cannibals cannot be this dang smiley. Jack is a total goocher. I sniff up the smell of the stew like I'm dying. Blue nods at it and I start eating as quickly as I can without being outright rude.

It tastes just as damn good as it smells. "This is delicious! I mean, almost as good as my mom's—" The words stick in my throat. Just talking out loud about her. And the way Blue is looking at me makes me want to burst out crying. I'm hit with all these feelings at once, like a thunderstorm out of nowhere. I want my mom here. I want Blue to meet her. I want to smell my mom. I want her to play with me like she used to. Mostly I just want a hug. I want to curl up in someone's lap and be held and rocked and not worry about anything.

I'm so angry at the damn Bleeds, I just go still. I brace up and freeze. Blue looks at me, caring and wise. I have to look down cause that look makes my eyes sting and my throat close up. Blue reaches out a hand and puts it softly on top of mine.

And I suck in air like I've been under water. I suck it in so I don't just start screaming, the ache is so big. Blue removes her hand slowly. I think she feels that it's too much.

"I'm sorry she's ill, Beckett," she says gently.

I start to get control. I nod. After I know I'm not gonna cry just yet, I speak. "Thanks, but she's going to be okay. Once Jack gets the right books to make the medicine to help her. Unless—do you guys have medicine here? Books on it?" I hold my breath, I'm hoping so hard. That would be so clutch. Then maybe Blue could meet her, and they would be friends, I know it—

"Only a few books to speak of. Those are a thing of the past, I'm afraid. And we only have the basic first aid and homeopathics here. We have doulas but they are only trained in birthing." Blue looks right sad. I know she's telling the truth. Just like I know she doesn't want my leg for her dessert. Before I can say anything else, Mateo is there, all eager and shiny-wet. He taps my shoulder and points. Seriously? I point the other way, and of course, he looks. I punch his arm.

"KNOCK, Mats. Grow up. GEEZ." I might have punched him a bit harder than needed. He grumbles something and sits down next to me. Logan, Digits, and Jack all follow. They're all dressed in the Underfolk gear and sweet smelling.

They seem older, somehow. It spooks me.

Logan clears his throat and looks at Blue. "Uhh, ma'am?"

"Call me Blue, son." She nods.

"Okay… Blue. Is that soap eatable?" Oh my GOSH—he's thick sometimes.

"Edible," Jack says before I can.

"SAME thing," Logan huffs then looks at Blue. "Uhh, is it… that?"

Blue smiles at him—not the same way she does me, and I like that. But still kindly. "Well, they're natural ingredients but nothing you would want on your dinner plate."

Logan points at Mats, grinning. "HA! Told ya so!"

Mats goes red-faced. "It's not poison, though, is it?"

Mateo ate the dang soap. Mucker. I'd be mad but he just looks so guilty, it's kinda funny.

"It won't hurt you, boy. Pretty sure it didn't taste all that great, though, right?" Blue smiles.

Mateo nods, a little less red.

The lady who served me comes back with a curly-haired boy and they have bowls of the stew for all of them. Jack is looking all strange at the boy, who puts the plates down and rushes off. Before I can ask him about it, everyone starts digging in like wild dogs. Everyone except for Jack. Mom taught us damn manners. I start kicking shins under the table. They flinch and glare but stop being all piggy. Folks continue to bustle around us. I can tell they're watching us, but anytime I look up at them, they smile. Not goocher smiles either. Real smiles.

"Have you lived here all your life?" Jack asks.

"Yes," Blue replies kindly.

"And you've never been above ground?" he continues between bites. I'm proud of his manners. He's taking his time, though I know he's starving.

Blue wipes her mouth. "On occasion. We have solar sheets hidden up top that we have to maintain."

"But that's it? How come you all ain't ghostly? Don't you need sun?" Logan says. That plonker! I move to kick him but he dodges. I see Digits grin at me out of the corner of my eye. I smile back.

"Well, sure. We all take turns up top for short spells; we just don't linger or mingle. And we make sure to eat the right stuff so we don't get too 'ghostly.' She smiles that laughing smile at him, even though she should whomp him.

"I'd go bonkers, never going outside to play," I chime in. Kind of wanting that smile back my way.

Got it. "I can see that. We get by all right, though. Do your parents know where you are?" she asks all of us.

"Hell's bells, lady—WE don't know where we are," Mateo mumbles through a bucketful of stew.

I can tell Jack is steamed at him by the way his shoulders are crunched up. "Chew with your mouth closed, Mats. And we do, so."

"And this store?" Blue presses.

"Bookstore," I pipe up. "The *last* one. It's got all the stuff we need to make the medicine Mom needs—"

Jack's shoulders crunch higher. "Becks," he cuts me off through gritted teeth. "I'm sure she doesn't want to hear all about it."

I open my mouth but Blue replies, "No, I'm very interested."

101

HA! I stick my tongue out at Jack and see his face go red. Double HA.

Blue interrupts my triumph. "I have heard talk of this store. But that's just it. Talk. Can't say as I've ever had actual proof."

Jack just stares down at his empty bowl and mumbles, "Well, we have." Rude. Not worse than Mateo's soap eating and stew guzzling, but still... rude.

"I'm sure. Otherwise, it would be a very big risk. I believe you're considering venturing into some very dangerous territory." She looks serious.

Mateo, who has been literally LICKING his bowl, blurts out, "Right!? Like, crazy with Blighters, ya know?! But that's cool—we got bombs and—"

Jack SLAMS his bowl down on the table. We all jump. Even Digits. It's silent for a beat as Blue just watches him. Not mad, just waiting. He exhales and looks up at her. "Miss Blue, I apologize. I'm just tired and worried about my mom. If it's okay, I'd just like to lie down for a bit?"

What the natch? Jack is never tired. Never. He's lying. Why is he lying?

Blue just smiles kindly at him. He gets up. As soon as he does, Logan springs up and stands beside him, as does Digits. Mateo is clueless because he's STILL got his face in that dang bowl. Never SEEN a bowl so clean. Digits finally smacks the back of his head. Mats looks up, sees Jack's face, and quickly gets up as well.

"Thanks for everything. That stew was way better than the soap," he says, stew covering his chin.

Blue nods. Then she looks at me and I feel my face smile back. "I can give you the rest of the tour if you want," she says. I grin bigger. Yes—maybe the nursery, and she can show me the—

`   I see Jack's face. He's glaring at me and all the boys are standing right with him. I'm about to tell them all to bug off when I see Digits's hand. "Just come," he signs.

I look in his eyes and he's got his serious face. There are few things I WON'T argue with. One of them is Dige's serious face. I look back at Blue, trying to cover my mad up. "I'd love that, but maybe later? I'm kinda wore out myself."

Blue smiles at me. It's extra wise and makes me want to take it back. "Sure thing, little one. We'll make it a plan." That just makes me madder at Jack and his busted look.

I follow them back toward the room. I wanna kick all of them—except Digits. I could never hurt Digits. As we reach the door, I grab Jack's arm. "What was THAT all about? You're being all—"

He SHUSHES me—which I HATE—and pulls me inside the room. The guys follow and close the door behind us.

"What's going on?" Logan asks. Finally, some sense coming outta that maw.

"We need to go," Jack says, all serious. WHAT?!

"But we just got—"

"Becks! For ONCE can you just NOT argue? Okay? Just trust me. Something is… off here." He's not mad at me, and that keeps me from just screaming at him. He seems… scared.

"What?"

"Where are the men?"

Well, that's just busted! I'm about to argue, then… wait… No, he's being crazy. "Well, there were all kinds of boys, right? You were even lookin' all plonky at one of 'em. And that guy—Blue's husband or whatever," I try.

Then Digits signs, "We were the oldest males in there other than him."

"Well, maybe they're all… working," I argue, because I just want Jack to see how nice Blue is.

"I don't think so. We've been here long enough for at least a few to come back."

I can't take it. "Aww, crap, you're just mad cause Blue likes ME better."

He shakes his head. "That's not it."

He's NOT LISTENING. I can feel my voice wanna yell. "They're NICE. They fed us and are letting us stay. You're ruining—"

"I can't really explain, okay? But we HAVE to get moving. We're running out of time."

And I stop. All I can see is my mom. Her face. Her bruises. Her pain.

I hate it when Jack's right.

Mateo suddenly turns to Jack, a crazy look on his face. "What if they don't let us go? Like, what if they really DO eat people—just all the men? What if we just ATE A BUNCHA DUDES they cooked!" He starts gagging and wiping his tongue on a blanket.

It would be a lot funnier if Jack laughed. But he's still wearing that grim face. "Just pack up. We're going to get out as soon as we can."

Chapter Twenty-One
Mateo

i mean, 1 second i'm eatin' that great soup, an' the next? All hell breaks loose.

First of all, i'm sick cuz Jack just told me we mighta eaten a bunch of man stew—then we're packed an' leaving, and i almost had a top bunk. Spanks that. Then again, i don't wanna end up stew 4 the next group of plonkers who wanders through.

Natch! I wonder if they had us wash with that clutch soap as like… seasoning?

We get our packs on an' Jack peeks out the door. There's a lot of noise out in the hallway. i can't tell what it's about, but Jack says, "Something's happening."

So i fart.

Can't help it. Sometimes my insides react 2 different happenings right quick.

"Jesus," Logan whispers.

"Sorry," i whisper back. Just wanting 2 get that man-stew taste outta my mouth. i peek out over Jack's shoulder and see a woman run by with a GUN. It looks old an' busted but it's STILL a GUN.

"We're going. NOW," Jack says.

He steps out in2 the hallway, all these women and kids runnin' all over. We walk all quick, in an' out of them down the hall. i'm keeping my eyes down so they don't all see how tasty i prolly am. Jack turns down another hall an' we stop an' look back. Again, cause i'm rear, i gotta lean out over Dige. i'm about 2 tell him 2 move when i see that lady Blue and the man-haired lady, Mel, walk up 2 our door. They're both holding weapons.

SEE! i knew they were wanting 2 eat us! "See, you guys—" i start, but then Logan's janky hand is over my mouth.

i shake him off but keep quiet cause now the dinner ladies are knocking on our door. An' it's not a "how ya doin'?" knock either. it's a "send out that plump one!" kinda knock.

Fart. Sorry.

i look back at them an' see that Blue lady pull out a HUGE knife and start jimmying our old door. My feet wanna run and Jack seems 2 agree cause he motions us down the hall, farther away from them. Again, we are in a line, keeping low, no eye contact as we all weave in an' out of them. i'm cleanup, so i just keep waiting 2 feel that huge knife in my back. Only thing keeping me from lookin' back all the time is havin' 2 watch Digits's back.

And that busted ol' goat is back.

i don't know why, but that stinky ol' thing just seems 2 LOVE Dige. Maybe it's a cannibal too? i try and shoo it away as we move thru everyone. Digits tries swatting at it, but it keeps tryin' 2 nibble at his pants.

DEFINITELY a cannibal goat. Natch that! I'm about 2 kick it when the world explodes. There's smoke an' dust, an' my ears are ringing. Digits turns back 2 me an' i see his mouth say: "BOMB!"

Rapid-fire farting. Sorry, sorry, sorry.

An' we are moving again. The goat takes off— guess it doesn't like bombs. i glance up an' see that one lady who let us in the big gates runnin' down the hall holding an AX in one hand an' a small kid in the other. Her face is dirty and a cut bleeds from her 4head. The little kid is crying. "You have 2 turn around—go 2 the NURSERY, now!"

Jack doesn't even pause, just looks up at her, thumbs up, an' says, "Sure! Right! Exactly!" An' leads us faster away. i hear her yellin' at us but just need 2 keep moving.

"STOP! You're going the wrong way!" she hollers, an' i look back 2 see Blue lady an' Man Hair comin' right our way.

So. Many. Farts.

"GO, JACK! They're comin'!" An' i push Digits 2 go faster. We are full-out running now.

BAM! Another bomb goes off, an' i have 2 peek up at Logan 2 see if it's his pack—i'm relieved 2 see he's not blown up. There's screamin' an' words flyin' all around my busted ears.

"North side—breached!" 1 yells.

"They're getting through!" Another.

"What is happening, Jack!?" Beckett. It's the scared in her voice that makes me speed up.

Run-run-run.

Logan dodges 2 the left an' looks down a hallway—shakes his head as he falls in line again. i see a door an' suddenly i just open it—didn't even know i was doing that. It's a room full of guys about our age, maybe older. They stare at me, all serious. One kid with hair so curly it looks like it's never been brushed stands up and says, "Run."

Dang, kid—don't gotta tell me twice. I slam the door closed an' push Digits harder.

Jack turns a corner an' we all run down a hallway. DEAD END. NATCHNATCHNATCH!

107

There's just a buncha old crates at the end. i turn around an' see Blue turn the corner.

Another lady runs up 2 her. "Start evac procedures?" she shouts 2 Blue.

Blue looks at us an' hollers back, "No. We can hold them. You get the children. I'll deal with this."

Beckett screams at Jack, "JACK! NOW!"

Jack looks all frozen 4 a second an' i start 2 wonder if they'll kill us be4 eating us, an' who is "breaching" what, an' what i would say 2 my mom if i could—

Jack starts moving boxes. Piling them on top of each other. "HELP ME!" he yells.

An' i'm pretty much throwing these huge crates, one over the other. Wherever Jack points. i look back as Blue is stopped by another woman yelling stuff.

MOVE IT.

We've got a huge pile of these crates now, an' Jack climbs up them 2 the top. There's boards on the ceiling an' he punches through 1. It isn't flimsy either. Has 2 hurt. Alls i see beyond that is black.

ANOTHER janky tunnel.

Crap.

Jack reaches his hand down 2 Becks. "BECKS, come on!"

Digits is there helping her, an' she disappears up in2 the black. Then Digits, then Logan. Jack, standing on the crates, reaches his hand out 2 me.

"Mats, MOVE IT! Come on!"

And i'm crawling up. i'm thinking how, just once, i'd like 2 be the guy helpin' everyone up 2 safety—when i look in2 the black.

i stop.

An' just when i was all admiring him, Jack shoves me through in2 it.

Chapter Twenty-Two
Logan

It's all janked. Janked to hell.

It's pitch black. We're crawling, and all I know is that Jack is behind everyone and Beckett is in the lead.

"STOP!" Jack shouts.

I barrel into Digits's rear. He grabs my hand and signs, "Okay."

I sign back the same and then add, "Beckett?"

He signs, "I have her. Here. Okay."

"OW! My GEMS, ya plonker!" Mateo yelps behind me. I hear rustling and grunting.

"It's just me. I'm coming up front." Jack steps on my ankle. I growl and he's past. "I think we are pretty far from—"

Just then we hear the sound of wood CRACKING from way back and distant voices.

Not distant enough. They are coming.

"Jack?" It's Beckett. I feel Digits pull his hand from mine and have a feeling he's grabbing hers. Whoa.

"Jack?" Beckett insists. Man, she can grate sometimes, but I swear, the sound of her afraid makes me feel... wrong.

"Okay, come on this way!" And I hear him start crawling. Leading us to... away... I don't know.

"Wait! You don't even know where you're going!" I say from behind Digits's butt. Did I mention how MUCH I HATE following people?

"You got a better idea?!" Jack shouts back, still crawling.

Beckett tries to stop us. "Both of you just—"

And suddenly there's someone else with us. I hear more than see them. All I can see is a kind of change in the darkness. I hear a landing and a small splash. I fumble in my pack 4 my torchlight—NATCH this—

Digits beats me to it, shining his in front of us. Jack's light joins it. Their torches crisscross until they settle on the figure.

It's a girl.

She's squatting in the pipe, facing us. A scarf covers her head, like the Underfolk. Her hands are shielding her eyes from the light. Digits and Jack lower the beams a little. She uncovers her face. She's dirty but you can tell she's pretty... More than that. She has these green eyes that seem like they glow.

And they're looking right at Jack.

Damn.

I know it's wrong, but I feel my neck heat up— mad at Jack. I've seen other girls look at him that way, and even though he hasn't kissed near as many as I have—hell, he hasn't kissed any... But that look. I've seen that look shot in his direction by more than one girl be4.

The girl breaks the stare and says, "It's this way, follow me."

And she starts crawling past us, <u>back</u> toward where we just were. Goocher green-eyed girl.

"No, we just came from there," Jack starts as she passes him.

"Just follow me or you're gonna die," she says without even turning back.

Jack won't budge. He holds out his hand, stopping Becks, and shines the light on the girl's back. "They're back there—you're going right into—"

She stops, all huffy like girls get, and looks at him, into his light. That look. "It's too small 4 most of them to get through. Now MOVE." But Jack just stares at her, a weird LOOK in his eyes. She stares back with HER look.

NATCH this.

"Or you could just go your way," she says. "See what that gets you." And she starts crawling again.

Digits shines his light toward Jack. We are waiting on his move.

Jack looks… weird. Like when you get kicked by a pig or thrown from a bike and your bell's rung. Stunned.

Then he moves.

And just like that, we're all following some janky, beautiful, green-eyed girl into the dark.

Chapter Twenty-Three
Digits

A new soldier.

She dropped from nowhere to lead us to... elsewhere. There is a look about her, in her eyes, that is familiar. It warms me, and I recognize that it is the feeling of *her*.

Beckett.

Only different. Not as warm. Not as uncontrollable, but... exhilarating.

I see the way the soldier looks at Jack, and he at her.

I know there is something grand at work here.

Of course, we have no choice but to follow. Just as I would follow Beckett to the end of the atmosphere and beyond.

Our choice has been made by greater forces.

Situation Report: On the move.

Status: Anxious but intrigued.

Chapter Twenty-Four
Avery

Her days of asking for a cure, for time, for strength… are over.

She knows what lies ahead. Now she just needs help to get through the next moment. Every day, she wakes and takes inventory of a new bruise, a new pain, a new blister. They are the physical notches that now mark her waning days, and they are adding up. Her time is running out. She knows she has to do this now or it will be too late.

"Please," she whispers.

It is a variation on a prayer to an unknown god that was passed on to her from her mom. She was told she could construct her own belief in her own god as she saw fit. "Just give it all the qualities that you would have in a best friend," her mom told her. "That way, you can just talk easy, like you would to an old friend."

This time, Avery's "please" is only for a little strength. A little help to get through this next task. She has to do this, and it has to be now. She inhales deeply and picks up the old quill, an anniversary gift from Reese. It is one of her favorite things.

"Don't you dare start crying. Not yet. Not yet." She steels herself, dips the pen, and begins to write.

Dearest Jack and Beckett,

There are just too many things I want to tell you and not enough time. I know that your dad will fill in anything I forget, so I want you to consider his words as if they are mine. I want you to know that you are my greatest treasures. My most significant contributions to this forming world of ours. You have given me the greatest joy of my life and made my journey here complete... Even if we feel it's too short.

You may grieve however you need to—it is grief, but it shows itself in varying ways for everyone—but I also want you to lean on each other for support. You are each other's greatest allies; please try to remember this in those times when you get so furious you can't see it. Be kind. To each other, to others, to yourselves. Lead with your heart. We have raised both of you to do so, and I expect you to maintain that, even when it's not convenient or comfortable. Remember, you are at your bravest when you are facing truly frightening things. Take time. Live in the moments. Stop. Pet the animals, see the sunrises, feel the wind on your faces, because it all matters... and it all goes so fast.

The tears begin in spite of her best efforts. She lifts her face away from the page, so as not to run the ink. She puts the pen down and holds her hands over her mouth, physically stifling the sobs that threaten. The tears spill out over her battered hands, her muffled agony audible to none.

"Please."

Xander

The smoke clears from the battle as the door to the underground city painfully slides open. Xander, Ash at his side, and a large group of Blighters behind him wait on the other side.
Armed and agitated.

Blue steps out, covered in dust and dirt. Gentry and Dolly flank her, wielding primitive but intimidating weapons. Behind them stands a larger group of Underground women. They are all dressed for battle and covered in debris.

All are armed.

Blue and Xander regard each other. Silent tension screams.

Blue speaks first. "That wasn't necessary."

"I disagree." Xander chuckles. His smile is disarming. "You know what I want."

"Xander, our agreement has been upheld. Stop this. You're shorting your own supply."

Xander sighs, as if talking to a petulant child. He is equally patronizing and chilling. "That sounds like a scolding, Blue. Are you scolding me?"

Gentry puts a hand gently on Blue's back. Warning her. Blue takes a deep breath. "What exactly do you want, Xander?"

"My progeny. You cannot shelter her anymore."

"She isn't here." Blue bites back her anger.

"Then everyone dies." He lifts a hand. Ash steps closer. The Blighters giggle and pulse forward.

"WAIT! Stop! Just... wait," Blue begs. She has worked too hard to protect her city. She cannot let it

come to this—no matter how painful the sacrifice. She turns and looks at Jamis, who nods and disappears back behind the door.

"Xander. I have… extra offerings this month. They are clean." She closes her eyes for a second, almost willing herself to make the inexcusable offering.

Jamis steps through the crowd with three BOYS, all bound and gagged. They are all shell-shocked except for a boy with curly hair, who looks right at Xander. Unflinchingly. Xander smiles at him—a possible general? He nods to Shadow, who steps forward and does a perfunctory inspection: hair, veins, lymph nodes. He nods. Clean.

Xander smiles brightly. "That's VERY nice, Blue. Thank you for this extra offering. I accept. Ash, will you please do the honors?"

Ash takes the restraining rope from Jamis and pulls the boys back to the Blighters' side. He silences their muffled cries with hard punches to their backs.

Blue looks away, stricken. She cannot forgive herself. She never can. But these offerings ensure that her people remain safe.

"And now, the girl," Xander presses.

"I told you! She isn't here!" Blue insists.

"Then death and mayhem are your only consolation." He stares into her eyes and begins to lift his hand.

"WAIT! You can take the food—fresh food, water, more… more donors. You could stay here—we have working systems, weapons, a full supply of donors at your… disposal. You could—"

"Stop, woman. Just stop."

Blue quiets, fighting back tears. She runs a kingdom yet must placate this monster.

"If I wanted this dirt hive, I would have taken it years ago. It's a stable for me. That is all. I'll find another. I believe our agreement is void at this time." He raises his hand and Ash screams and runs forward, knocking aside everyone in his path. A wave of insane Blighters follows in his wake, entering the protected underground city.

"STOP," Blue screams.

Xander whistles and his people freeze in their tracks. He waits. Blue reluctantly reaches into her pocket and pulls out a piece of flowered cloth. Xander grabs it and inspects it, a small smile growing on his face. He holds it up to his nose and inhales deeply.

"I'm the only one who knows where she went. Stop this. Leave. I'll... I'll show you where." Blue looks at him, defiant.

"Make your choice."

Chapter Twenty-Five
Jack

We've been crawling through these plonky tunnels behind that girl forever. The girl. She looks my age but her eyes… they seem much older. Like they've seen things a kid shouldn't. Makes me both sad and… intrigued to look at them. "Where are we going?" I ask.

"Where we need to go," she says, not stopping.

I've had just about all I can take of these mucker tunnels, Mateo's busted whining, and the girl's damn answers and weird eyes. I'm opening my mouth to tell her as much when we suddenly come into a larger tunnel junction. It's big enough for us to stand, and everyone gets up and bumps into each other trying to stretch our busted legs. I hold up my torchlight and look around. It leads out to four separate tunnels. Suddenly, I'm not as irritated with her. I wouldn't want to guess which one we need. I don't even try.

"Which way now?" I ask.

She steps toward the center of the space and reaches down to a big steel manhole.

"Little help?" she says, looking at all of us. I wonder if anyone else thinks her eyes are… Logan steps up quickly because he's a competitive goocher, but I am suddenly right there next to him, pulling the giant thing up and to the side. There's just blackness underneath it. But it's big. I can tell from the blast of cold air and the way our voices echo.

"So there's a… slight drop before you land. Just keep your arms and legs together," she says, LOOKING at me with those eyes.

"Land where?" I say, because I sure as natch am not going to—

BOOM! An explosion goes off somewhere. Not close, but not far enough away to stay here arguing.

The girl looks at me. "Safety." She says it simply, but it seems like there's a lot more behind those words.

I hoist my legs in without a word. Not because I'm brave but because I really don't trust my voice not to do some janky crack or something if I try and talk right to her. I'm about to let go, but that cold air. That echo…

"Just curious, how 'slight' is the dr—"

AND SHE PUSHES ME.

I fall for about three seconds, but in pitch-black-falling-through-space-time that feels like a LOT longer. I land hard and remember to bend my knees and roll. Mid-roll, I'm wondering if I'm going to drop into some other free fall, but I'm too angry to stop. Once I feel like I'm on safe ground, I shine my torchlight upward. "I'm okay! And that girl is NATCH!"

I'm shining the light right AT her damn smiling face. She motions for the others, and they drop down one by one. She is the last.

Once we are all down, Logan and I shine our lights around. It looks like an old storage closet or something. There are dusty, broken shelves along one wall, a file cabinet along another, and in the corner, a worn bedroll, some tattered blankets, and water in containers. Someone's been living here.

The girl crosses to the bed, pulls out a canteen, and drinks from it. She offers it to Becks, who takes it and drinks. Suddenly, I want to ask the girl a million questions.

120

She lives here? Where is her family? How does she get food? Is she trustworthy?

She turns and stares at me. Defiant. Like she can hear every single thought I'm thinking.

"Who are you?" I try and squeak out, even though I feel like I don't have any air.

"The one who just saved you." She stashes the canteen back behind the bedroll.

Damn, she's... well, snotty, yes, but something else. Something kind of... interesting. I don't have time to answer because... well, Mateo.

"See! I TOLD you they were going to eat us!" he yells.

"Who's going to eat you?" the girl asks.

"Them Underfolk! They eat all the men!" he yelps before I can stop him.

Beckett sighs loud and long. "Mats, will you just shut your trap? You'd taste like dust farts anyway!"

Mateo looks at the girl with his hands out, as if to say, "Am I right?" and no one can argue because, well, we'd really like to know once and for all if we just escaped being a main course.

The girl just looks at each of us. Her face unreadable. I thought Blue was hard to read—the girl is impenetrable.

The. Moment. Drags. On. Forever. My stomach starts to go plonky, my eyes burn... HOW IS MATEO NOT INTERRUPTING RIGHT NOW? Then, slowly but amazingly, she smiles. It starts small, at only the corners of her eyes, then spreads to her mouth and then her whole face. It's one of those smiles that, like a yawn, is helpless to resist.

I feel the smile burst onto my face. I know it's goofy but I'm helpless to stop it.

"So they don't eat the men, right?" I say through that janky grin. Everyone else has relaxed and is smiling that same huge smile. Like a virus. The girl, still smiling, shakes her head no. I want more answers, though.

"Where were they?" I demand, trying to stop my own goofy grin.

"Who?" She's smiling at me. Wow. What?!

"The men?" I squeeze between my huge teeth. I am smiling bigger now. Stop. IT.

"There aren't any. 'Cept Gentry and the kids," she says plainly. She won't look away. I feel like there's something in my chest that feels… magnetized. To her. I know that's crazy, but in this moment, I'm SURE she is feeling the same thing. She won't look away from me. Those eyes.

Of course, Logan is the one to ruin it. PLONKER! He actually steps up between us so she has to look at him!

"Why? How come those are the only men?" Why is he standing so close to her?

She steps to the side slightly so I can see her, and speaks to both of us. Ha!

"Just their way. Always has been." I can feel Logan wanting to block her view of me again. I scowl, wondering if I should just throttle him. She mistakes the look for doubt. "Well, why would they need them? If you want a peaceful, safe place, why even consider them?"

"Makes total sense to me," Beckett chimes in, and I'm actually grateful for once. Gets me a moment to catch my breath. "No conflict," Becks continues. "Men are predisposed to pillage and fight." She steps up to the girl. I take back what I said about being grateful. Now she's ganging up on us with a stranger!

Logan takes the bait before I can. "You're predisposed to kiss my ass," he mumbles. Great. Real clutch, Logan.

"See?" Becks says, looking at the girl and motioning toward Logan. What?! I can't take it—Becks is also blocking my view.

I step up. "Can you explain, please? Cause it's my thinking that a village full of WOMEN would bring nothing but conflict." I keep my face blank as she meets my eyes. Again.

She steps closer. "You're wrong. They have a safe, working order. A council, headed by Blue and Gentry—"

"How come he gets to stay?"

"He's Blue's man. But as equal as everyone else." She squares her shoulders. We are the same height.

"But the kids?" I counter. "How—"

"Some of the women have... agreements with some traveling folks. They can stay over when they pass through. Just for a night, though."

Suddenly, we both become very aware of how close we're standing. We're frozen. Well, I am, and I can see she's not moving or looking away or—

"But why would—oh," Beckett realizes out loud.

The girl and I are both able to take a slight step away and break eye contact. I'm relieved and... sad?

Mateo strikes. "AWK-ward."

I smile, happy to have a reaction that seems natural for a moment. Digits steps up to Logan and begins signing. Logan interprets—for the girl mostly. Mucker. "He says that Blue was talking about getting us out. Mel just wanted to 'end this once and for all.'"

Wait. What? "So they weren't going to kill us?" I ask Digits. He shakes his head. "Oh, but then…" I can't sort everything out. Did I just put everyone in more danger? I turn to the girl, hoping for answers. "What was going on down there?"

She looks away. Still can't read her. "Blighters," she says. "Normally, they don't ever cross each other. They have a truce. This is bad. They're afraid of the Underground… usually." It's troubling her, that much I can tell. I don't want to press her on it.

"So… you got a name?" I ask. Willing her to stop being sad. To look at me again.

"Nyx. It's short for—"

"Phoenix. The bird that rose from the ashes," I say, smiling. Because I know. Because I like it. Because she's looking at me again.

"No. Just Nyx. It's short for Nyx," she says. Her face is blank as she stares at me.

Then I see it. The edges of her eyes first, then her mouth. The smile. Of course, my goocher goofy grin shines right back. And we're stuck again.

Beckett coughs. Obvious. We both glance away. Thank you and damn you, Beckett.

"Well, I'm Beckett, Jack's sister—that guy with the plonky grin. And that's Logan, who thinks he's the best at everything. Digits, his brother, who can't talk but sees and knows everything. And Mateo, who farts when he's scared but can lift a horse," she says. Digits sports my same goofy smile at Beckett, even though everyone else is scowling at her.

Mateo tries, "Well, you're Beckett—"

"Just said that—" Becks replies.

"Who… who's a—a goochy mucker… a butt licker… bossy…" he stammers. Everyone, including Nyx, starts smiling at his struggle.

"Careful, Mats—you're gonna sprain something," Logan says.

"Awww—all you guys are busted," Mats blurts, but he doesn't concede. He turns to Nyx. "I happen to be… great. At all things. There."

Nyx smiles and nods. This seems to work. Mats nods in reply and walks back beside Digits.

"Listen," I say. "I have no idea where we are or if we're in danger, but we have to get—"

But she's already busy pushing the busted-out file cabinet to the side. What is she doing? I step up behind her and see that the cabinet was hiding something.

A door. An old, thick door. She flips a latch and opens it, then steps to the side. Before Logan can, I step up and shine my torchlight into the space.

"Holy crap," is all I can choke out.

Chapter Twenty-Six
Beckett

I feel all the air leave my body.

Mom calls us "extraordinary" sometimes. She uses it when she's proud of Jack or me, and it's usually about something good. I guess I always just took the word itself for granted, but that's all I can think as I stand here looking around at this place. Extraordinary. It is. It feels like somewhere from a different world, and I suppose it is. This place has been forgotten. By time. By people. By a war that we talk about and study in school. Something that, no matter what people tell us, is only a story to us. But this place, this huge, breathtaking, extraordinary place, is just that. EXTRA-ordinary. It feels like MORE than our lives. Our home. Our town. Our world. Just MORE.

There's a giant open ground floor. Everywhere I can see is lined with shelf after shelf, all packed fat with BOOKS. Old, new, colorful, faded. There are huge archways and tunnels BUILT FROM BOOKS. Like it was the only material they considered to make barriers, tunnels, rooms. There are crazy angles to the structures, but they're also so… precise. Each book creating another brick in the form.

All of it… beautiful. Magical. Perfect. Extraordinary.

There's a small stage and performance area in front. A counter with candles and paintings—SO MANY paintings on almost every square inch of wall. Some scary and swirling and dark. Some so beautiful, I want to swim in them. No real theme or pattern to them, but they all seem to work. I'm struck by all the care and feeling that went into these... so long ago. By people who had no idea they would still affect one small girl so many, many years and worlds later. I wish I could thank them. I can see up into the open second and third levels through the ironwork railings. Every space is more books, creating mazes and archways and leading to rooms... so many rooms, and that's just what I can see from down here.

There are big worn couches and huge comfy chairs all over. Placed by people long ago who knew that once a space like this was created, you would just want to settle in and stay, so they made it comfortable and possible to do so. "Settle in," the couches seem to say. "You're going to want to stay."

And I do. Oh... how I do.

Somehow I find my breath and step forward. I guess my mouth has been hanging open because I can taste dust and... age. It smells old, I guess, but not in a bad way like Mr. Ganner at the general goods store. This smells old in a ... wise way? I dunno—I just know it's not bad at all and I don't mind the taste of wise on my tongue.

I see Jack step slowly up beside me, his mouth hanging open in just the same way. Breathing in all the wise. He looks over at Nyx, who seems to be the only one of us not struck openmouthed-goocher right at the moment.

"How did you...?" Jack squeaks out.

She looks a little embarrassed. "I was tracking you guys. Sound carries. Sometimes I... helped. Like with the rats. I kind of herded them one way to stop you from going the wrong way. I... come here. I have places. This one's my best. Until now, that is." She crosses over by the checkout counter and pulls out an old box filled with more candles. Jack steps up and they begin lighting them and placing them all around. The glow makes it feel even more alive. Like the color of the place's... heartbeat.

I. Can't. Take. It. Anymore.

With my torchlight and some candles in hand, I bolt for the corner spiral staircase—I HAVE TO SEE!

"Beckett! Wait!" Jack yells behind me. But I simply have to see every corner. I have to make sure it's even real.

"It's okay—there's no other way in," I hear Nyx tell him. "And no one's been here in... a while." She is also extraordinary. I knew this the first moment she dropped down into that tunnel. Of course she would end up leading us here.

I twist around and around, up, up, up the curling steps, watching as mine are the only footprints made in thick layers of dust. I hear Dige, Logan, and Mateo all running for different areas, all of them now laughing and playing around. It's like when you turn out a foal on a crisp, cool morning after being cooped up all night.

It's the sound of freedom. It's joy. It's our giant, living pasture of hope. I feel kind of weird, like when Mom makes me take valerian root or something for a cough—woozy but also funny and warm. It's a good feeling, but not exactly in control.

"Natch control!" my feet say and move even faster. I hit the second floor and am twisting and turning through more books and arches and mazes. I hear weird giggles coming from somewhere and I realize they're mine. I break for the railing to call down to Jack but then I see him and Nyx talking. I duck a little, just out of sight.

"I swear. It's not a trap. It's safe here," Nyx is promising. They're standing really close together. "After the Darkening, no one needed books, just weapons and food. When the Blighters took control, they destroyed anything they didn't want. The whole front of this place is covered in rubble. Over time, people who knew about it just died off."

She seems comfortable but not exactly at home. Jack is looking around at things, taking it in… but his focus is mostly on her. "How do you know all this, then?"

"My mom. Before she died, she'd tell me stories. That's how I knew it'd be safe." She starts to move. They're kind of circling each other. I don't think they know it. The circles get a little smaller but the space between them seems… magnetized.

"So you live here?" he asks her. Dang—I sure would. It would be the greatest!

"I… come here. Don't really live anywhere," she says plainly. So plainly it makes my heart hurt a little. I see Jack look at her, then they both look away. Plonky boys. He should hug her. I feel like I want to. He wanders over to a corner, and I see that it's another separate space. A bedroll is set up with old blankets and a pillow, some food, a water jug. Right above it is this weird statue thing, like the kind they used to show clothes in the old days, but it's only the top half. It's a woman's body and head. Her torso has been painted with bright swirls and flowers all over, except her face. There's a yarn wig for hair and candles placed all around it.

It's an altar. I know this from the Lander's End Church—which Dad says we could go to if we want, but we only went once because it's so dang boring, even when they sing.

I stand because, dang it, if Jack isn't going to hug this girl, I will—even if she doesn't know she needs it.

He takes a step toward her. Maybe he's not so thick after all. I feel that weird magnet thing again.

"Jack! There are like a billion books! More than even YOU could read!" Logan's mucker voice breaks their magnet, and Jack and Nyx step back from each other. Logan stands across the way from me on the second floor. GOOCHER. He keeps talking, cause he's thick as mud. "There's a Science Fiction room, a Mystery room—anything you're looking for, you can find!" Then I see Digits pop out from behind a shelf and come to the railing. He signs something down to Jack about a "Weapons and Defense room," and his eyes are all lit up and his hands are moving so fast that I almost can't read them. He looks… alive. I feel a big grin break out on my face. Then I blush. *What?* I stand up, about to wave at him, when suddenly I hear Mateo scream.

I jump back and duck, trying to hear where it came from. Who's here!?

He calls down from the railing on the third floor. "There's, like, a LOT of pictures up here with NAKED LADIES! A LOT!" he screeches.

Before I can yell at him, I see Logan in a full-out run, trying to get up there to see painted boobs faster than a greased pig.

Boys. Are. Janky.

Natch this. I'm going to keep exploring. I feel almost panicked that I won't see everything soon enough. There're so many corners, so many twists and shelves and rooms...

And I find it.

It's a smaller room, almost hidden, but I see an old cross, like a medical cross, next to a stethoscope above the door. I walk in and look around. There's a statue with its whole front cut off, showing all the veins and organs—you can even take them out. It's a model of the human body. There are cabinets and drawers of old medical instruments and apparatuses.

My heart starts beating faster.

I look at the walls—all of them are lined floor to ceiling with books, and I start reading titles. I touch them, my fingers moving as fast as my brain can read. My breath catches. This. Ohhhh... this. The tears hit my hand before I know I'm crying. I walk out of the room on feet that don't seem like my own, and I cross to the railing. "Jack. Come here," is all I can choke out.

I wander back toward the room, standing there to motion him in. He's there in seconds, with Nyx right behind him. I guess my voice scared him. I motion them into the room and step in behind them. He starts looking around and reading the book titles. He reaches out to touch one but snatches his hand back. As if he's afraid it will vanish if he touches it.

I can feel him holding his breath.

"They're all medicine books, Jack. ALL OF THEM. From blood to heart to treatments and surgeries… Everything. Right here," I whisper through the tears. "You did it, Jack. This is it."

He turns and looks at me like he's just come back from a dream. His eyes are glassy.

We stare at each other, and I swear a silent oath in that moment that I would lay down my life for him, I love him so much. He just looks at me. He nods his head. I know he can't speak. It's somehow too big. Too much. Gotta fix this…

"Course, you'd be coyote poop if it weren't for me." I smile, plonky tears still dripping off my chin. He grins.

There's a tiny cough behind him, and I remember that Nyx is there. She looks a little embarrassed, like she's been spying. "It—it's what you wanted?" she asks.

All I can do is hug her. So I do. I hug her so hard. I feel her body tense at first, like it's scary, but as I sniffle and nod my head against her shoulder, I feel her body relax. She's not hugging back, but it shifts. There's a physical… opening that I can feel.

The feel of a smile.

I step back and let her have her space. She looks away, hiding the last wisp of the smile.

"It's perfect," I tell her.

Jack is devouring the books now. Pulling out one after the other, opening it, reading, going for another, reading titles, moving from row to row. It's like when Mom sets out sugared dates for us and we know there're only so many.

"There's everything. Apothecary, homeopathy, modern disease—well, 'modern' for back then, anyway," he says, his voice fast and high.

I look on and turn to Nyx. "How come you don't just live here? There's so much."

"Found it a few years ago and... I dunno, I just come to stay sometimes. It seemed... strange, somehow. Like a different world," she says with a shrug. I understand because of the extraordinary thing, but there's something else in her face.

"A sacred place," Jack says quietly. It's spooky sometimes, how he and I think alike.

Nyx shrugs again, her expression hard. "I don't know. I just never... had much use for books."

Oh.

Jack is looking at her and she looks back at him. It's that magnet thing again, but I just don't have time for that because I. Am. So. Dang. Excited.

"I can teach you!" I blurt. Magnet breaks. She turns to me.

"Teach me what?" she says, her shoulders rising again.

"How to read!" I feel her shift, but I also feel like I can't stop the words coming from my face. I just want to get started. I want to help her. I want to show her all the—

"I know how to damn read! I can read all I need. I know 'up,' 'down,' 'left,' 'right,' 'over,' 'under,' 'danger,' 'exit'... and other words. Lots of words!" she bites out.

CRAP. FIX IT, BECKETT, I hear my brother thinking at me. I even glance at him to make sure his mouth didn't move, and his eyes are saying EXACTLY THAT. I gentle my tone, like you do with a skittish pup. "I have so many things to show you—like stories and other worlds. Cars and adventures. Other times, places! Sometimes there's mushy stuff, like kissing, but also GREAT stuff, like video games and television and—"

"Beckett, ease up—" Jack says, trying to calm me, but I feel that word-tumbling thing building up again…

"How the hell are a buncha words gonna help ANYTHING?!" Nyx shouts, all defensive. "I mean, is a kissing book gonna help me stay alive? Which of these stories is gonna give me food? Water? I don't need your stories, understand? I have my own—I have—" She suddenly stops. She looks at Jack and me, crazy mad, then just turns and storms out.

I'm frozen. My words want to spill out after her. My brain keeps trying to shout things and my feet are stuck to the ground, trying to decide who to listen to. I look at Jack.

"Don't do it. I mean it, Becks. Just give her a—"

NATCH THAT.

My feet are moving.

Chasing that extraordinary girl.

Chapter Twenty-Seven
Mateo

Boobs. Like… everywhere.

So.

Many.

Boobs.

Oh, an' couches—great, huge couches. Going 2 make a cushion tower like 17 stories high.

Chapter Twenty-Eight
Logan

This place is so CLUTCH.

There are books everywhere, which isn't usually my thing, but they are built into whole rooms and tunnels and statues. There's stuff in every corner. I'm real happy for Jack—and all of us—that we found it. I want to show him the lady pictures too, but...

Well, he and that girl haven't really left each other's side.

They look at each other... and it's <u>that</u> look.

I found a case thing with old candy in it and shook one out called S-N-I-C-K-E-R-S and tried to eat it, but it was all gray and mostly dust. Was going to share it with Jack but... Nyx. Damn. I'm trying to be happy, though. We made it. That's swank.

I see Digits kind of spying on Becks. Nothing new there. Mateo is throwing, like, every cushion from every couch down to the center of the ground floor. I'm just wandering around.

I should feel happier.

Last summer, Jack told me that he had a crush on Teelah. I tried to help him talk to her but... well, he gets that thing where he starts babbling when he's nervous, so he just wouldn't. One day, after leaving his house, I saw Teelah in town. I didn't need to, but I went into the merchant's where she was. Started talking to her. I kissed her that day. Out behind the motor shop. I didn't even really want to, and I never spoke to her after.

I also never told Jack. But I think he knows.

Right after I kissed her, I felt the same way as I do now, watching Jack and Nyx look that weird look at each other.

Chapter Twenty-Nine
Digits

Nyx has delivered us to our target destination. The outcome is greater than I had hoped for in my most ambitious wishes. The bookstore is formidable. Breathtaking. Alive. Every corner holds a secret. A revelation. An adventure. So many corners pull me. So many titles seem to swell forward as I pass, begging me to open their stiff, lonely spines and drown in the knowledge that floods out.

And there is Beckett.

I have no recall for sound. I have known only the flash of fingers and the nuance of the mouth since I was a baby. I try to imagine sound: a dog's bark, a baby's cry, thunder, laughter, birdsong, a moto-bike… Even with a vast vocabulary and descriptive mind, words fail me. How would a blind person describe the color red?

Sometimes I get frustrated at having no reference.

But never as much as when I watch *her.*

I cannot imagine her voice, but I sometimes believe it would sound like the sunrise looks.

Beckett is seated in the medical room with a leather-bound version of *To Kill a Mockingbird* in her lap. Jack is there, fixated on scanning and selecting texts. Nyx inspects the medical dummy and tries to observe, while remaining on guard. Mateo is jumping from the second story onto his pillow mountain and Logan is brooding near enough to watch Jack and Nyx orbit each other.

Becks reads the words and feels the pages with tender awe. She's choosing selections to read aloud to

Nyx, who pretends not to listen but maintains rapt attention.

I secure myself behind a nearby stack, peeking through at Beckett's mouth. Her words. Their shape. Imagining the hues and weight of the clouds and light that burst from her in sound.

It's what I imagine music would feel like in the ears.

"Atticus said to Jem one day, 'I'd rather you shot at tin cans in the back yard, but I know you'll go after birds,'" her lips sing. *"'Shoot all the bluejays you want, if you can hit 'em, but remember it's a sin to kill a mockingbird,'"* she reads as if she were a priest and it a scripture.

"That was the only time I heard Atticus say it was a sin to do something and I asked Miss Maudie about it. 'Your father's right,' she said. 'Mockingbirds don't do one thing but make music for us to enjoy. They don't eat up people's gardens, don't nest in corncribs, they don't do one thing but sing their hearts out for us. That's why it's a sin to kill a mockingbird.'"

Beckett pauses and looks up at Nyx as if all the secrets of the Universe have been revealed. Her eyes glisten with the reverence, the scope of it. My chest aches and Nyx smiles at her, caught up as I am in Beckett's symphony. She pages through the book some more, unapologetic, inspired. "I don't know what corncribs are, but I've seen pictures of mockingbirds... Atticus was the greatest..."

She sifts through and Nyx is enchanted. Waiting, as I am. At this point, Mateo and Logan have wandered close, standing in the doorway. I move from my hiding spot and join them. An audience, waiting on its next treasure. We are rewarded. "Listen to this," and she reads, *"I wanted you to see what real courage is, instead of getting the idea that courage is a man with a gun in his hand. It's when you know you're licked before you begin, but you begin anyway and see it through no matter what.'"*

It is so silent I'm afraid the others will hear my heartbeat.

Suddenly, a tear drops onto the page Beckett holds. She looks up in time to see Nyx quickly wipe her eyes. Nyx, suddenly self-aware, sees the rest of us looking on. She focuses on Jack, then stands and bolts past us faster than even Beckett can react.

Beckett moves to pursue her, but Jack holds up his hand, stopping her. "I got it. You guys try and find a way to carry out all the books I piled outside the reference room. We gotta get back."

He pursues her. As if he ever had a choice.

I look at Beckett. Wanting her to read more. Wanting her to smile. Wanting her to hear all the things I cannot adequately say with only two hands.

Situation Report: Holding.

Status: Sheltered in place. Exposed from within.

Chapter Thirty
Reese

There was blood on those rocks.

He rides beside Garrett, both pushing their horses faster than safe or possible.

There was blood on the rocks.

It wasn't a lot… but still blood. They tracked the children to the tunnel to the Underground and, trying to time out their travel, decided to ride through to the city to try and head them off.

There was blood on those rocks.

He pushes his horse faster. The thunder of hoofbeats and labored breathing almost drowns out his thoughts.

Almost.

Garrett thinks he knows a back way into the city center. Where they won't have to encounter too many Blighters. Reese prays he is right. They are as armed as they can be. Fueled by fear, fury, and a single phrase.

My kids. My kids… My KIDS.

They crest a hill and the city looms.

Xander

The Blighters and the Underfolk remain frozen, waiting for Xander's decision.

Xander finally removes the fabric from his nose. Her sweet stench still lingers on the worn cloth. He turns to Shadow. "Take them. Now. If anyone disobeys, there will be consequences."

The Blighters turn en masse and disappear, following Shadow back through the tunnels.

Xander waits until the last of them is gone then smiles at Blue. "As you were saying."

"The bookstore... I've only heard rumors of it, but that's where she stays. She goes through the tunnels to get there. They're too small for a normal-sized adult."

"What about the front entrance?"

"Rubble. Completely buried. That's why it's gone abandoned for so long."

Xander motions to Ash. "That's fine. I have a human wrecking ball. You will show me the way around."

Blue is about to argue. Her affection for the girl is longstanding and deep despite the lack of genetic connection.

"Show me, or I harvest every last child in these walls."

The bodies are his crop, to be used for blood and then abandoned like empty cornhusks.

Blue hangs her head, broken. She has become a farmer of souls. For him.

Inside, she knows her only salvation is to save the girl. And the group. She silently resigns herself to do so… or die trying.

It must end.

Chapter Thirty-One
Jack

When Becks was about five, we were in town with my mom. We were just waiting outside
the general store and we heard this whining. I looked around but couldn't see anything. We weren't supposed to leave the front of the store.

Of course, Becks took off after the sound. I followed her as she ran toward the back of the store and just stood there, really still. I was about to tell her how much trouble she was going to get into when that whine came again. At first, I thought it was a cat or something because it was so small and muddy, all curled up by a compost barrel. Shivering and whining.

Hurt. Left in a corner, shaking and alone.

Becks approached it, hand out, talking low. I was scared that it would bite her, so I stepped up next to her. It was a dog. It had been beaten or wild or something, and it didn't look good. Its ear was torn, and it was skinny and scared. I wanted to go get my mom but Becks just leaned down, talking low and soft, and put out her hand. The dog looked like it was going to bite her, but it sniffed and then licked her, whining. Then Becks just opened her hands and that tiny dirt-caked thing just went right to her. He's our dog now. His name is Boo and he's about the greatest animal you'd ever want to know.

Nyx reminds me of Boo.

I don't mean she's like a dog or anything. Just that they are creatures that have seen and been through more than any soul should. But there's still the need to love, just waiting for the hand extended to give them the opportunity.

I finally find her in an upper room. It's all paintings and art pieces, like sculptures and glass forms. Everything is covered in dust, but it still reflects the candlelight, and the colors spin around in a kind of slow-motion wave. Nyx is standing by a hanging stained-glass mobile, gently tapping the pieces and making the colors swirl. I stand in the doorway, unable to move or speak. If she knows I'm here, she doesn't let on.

So I watch her. My mind is reeling and my chest is aching to let her know we are safe. That she doesn't have to be hurt or alone anymore. That I will keep her safe. I open my mouth and am just about to say something, anything, when she lifts her hand to the glass, and I see it: Her entire arm is covered in bruises and sores.

Hurt. Left in a corner, shaking and alone…

I guess I gasp or something because she spins around really fast, looking at me. Angry.

I step forward, holding out my hands and talking real soft like Becks did to Boo so many years ago. "Geez, Nyx, what the—"

And she bolts, shoving me aside.

So much for that approach.

So I chase her. She's running through the aisles, in and out of rooms and tunnels. She is fast and knows the layout, but I am determined, and after growing up chasing a janky little sister, I'm pretty good at anticipating moves and keeping up. We fly up staircases and down, under alcoves and through more aisles…

Damn, this place is big.

She makes to turn up another aisle, but I cut her off, forcing her to turn the opposite way— and BANG! I got her. She's cornered in a smaller children's reading room. She stops and spins, looking at me with those amazing fierce green eyes. Challenging.

I put my hands up and try to speak, but I'm pretty sure I am going to pass out. I'm wheezing and panting like a horse run hard. She's winded too, but not half as much. She looks trapped, like she's about to bolt again. I know my lungs can't take it.

"Truce. Okay? I'm gonna break my neck or burst a lung… Just… just stop a second, okay?" I pant. Her eyes still dart around, looking for an escape. "Okay, look, you don't have to tell me anything. You don't even have to stick around, okay? We're really thankful that you got us here." My breathing is finally returning to something mildly human. I try and think of all the right things to say, but it's like a dust storm of thoughts in my head, and when I look at her, scared, waiting, ready to disappear, they just sort of gush out. "Just so you know, we're leaving here—to get these books back and save my mom. But where we come from… it's safe. There's sunlight—well, except for at night. Anyway, you can come with us if you want. You and your family?"

At the word "family" she flinches.

Crap.

"Or just you. I mean… you could stay with us or whatever, or with someone else." I am now pacing in front of her because I've lost it. That babbling thing? It's not just Beckett. I think it may be a family trait. I feel my mouth still going, that storm of words spilling out. "I'm just saying you'd be welcome. We would like it if you wanted to come with us. You can do whatever you want. That's your thing, I get it… But, you know…" NATCH! I can't stop it.

But she is still there. She's staring at me. I can't read her expression. It's taking everything in my power not to vomit out more stupid words. She steps a little closer, staring at me with those unreadable green eyes. I can't move.

"So is it your town? Or all the books?" she says.

"What?" I say, inside and out.

"Wondering what makes you babble on like such a fool." She steps really close and then exits the room. In those few seconds, I see it.

She's smiling.

Damn.

When my breath returns to my body, I call to her back, "It's neither, for your information. It's a choice! I choose to…"

I'M SUCH A GOOCHER. I walk back the way we came. Not seeing her anywhere, I just head back to the medical room. Least I can do is make myself useful. Of course, Beckett is standing there, waiting on a full report.

"Well?" she asks, hands on hips.

"Well, what?" I start packing up books, not ready to admit my ultimate goocher-ness.

"Did you fix it? Is she okay?"

Dang, that girl can dig in. I take a moment to think as I pack and sort books. Mateo is here, smelling the medical dummy's organs. He seems occupied but Becks won't wait. I finally say, "She's… been hurt. By

147

someone. I think Blue and the Underfolk experimented on her or… I dunno."

Beckett stares at me, ready to cry. I know how she feels. It's Boo, but bigger. Harder. Before she can make it worse, I continue. "Look, I told her she could come with us. Back home. That she could stay."

Beckett smiles and hugs me. "What'd she say? Is she coming? Is she gonna?"

"I don't know. She's… quiet. But we have to get back, Becks. We can't mess around here, okay?" The clock is ticking, as my dad would say. Always ticking.

Beckett is happy with the possibilities. "I'm gonna go tell her how home is. I'll lie about you and your side of the room, of course."

Before I can stop her, she bolts in search of Nyx and those possibilities. I stand there, just trying to brace up for what lies ahead.

Chapter Thirty-Two
Beckett

I'm running to get Nyx, to tell her all the things about our town and animals and home. I'm bursting with all the good that I want to give to her and—

There's a BIG EXPLOSION.

The front of the store is a bunch of falling rocks. I turn to run. To find Jack. And suddenly…

I'm AIRBORNE.

Someone is lifting me up and grabbing me away. I know it's not one of us because it HURTS. I SCREAM. I'm bouncing down an aisle—I just feel huge arms around me, squeezing so hard. And the SMELL. Like rotted garbage and pain. I kick my feet and twist and squirm like a snake that's been stabbed. I hear a deep GRUNT and my legs are hobbled by an arm. We're moving quickly down another aisle, toward the stairs.

I see Jack run out of the medical room and dive to the ground. *PLEASE stay hidden.* There's a hand clamped over my screaming mouth, and I try not to gag at the smell. I'm being janked around so hard that it's tough for me to see, but I see small forms scrambling—the boys. They take cover. *HIDE-HIDE-HIDE.* I lose sight of them as I'm carried down the stairs, my hand hitting the railing hard. I wince as I try and twist, but I'm stuck. Whoever's carrying me lets out small bursts of grunts and giggles.

It is the sound of insanity.

Suddenly, we're at the bottom and I'm swung roughly down to the floor. I hit my head and my teeth ring together. I look up and see—

Nyx.

She's standing there in the middle of the room with a rope around her neck and her hands tied behind her back. Behind her is a tall, scrawny, filthy...

Blighter.

He pulls on the rope around her neck and she looks at me. Her eyes scream hurt, regret, and apology all at once. She is not as scared as I am, and I understand in that moment that this is not unusual for her. The tears threaten harder. Before I can speak, there's a rope around my neck. I'm yanked up by it and I grab for it, trying not to choke. I hear the giggling behind me as my hands are pulled behind me and tied. I glance back and see a short, goblin-like Blighter. He giggles through a mouth filled with black decay and three teeth. I gag again. He yanks my hands up, hurting my already swollen arm. NATCH THIS!

"I'M GONNA KILL YOU!" I scream.

"Spirited." The voice is deep and dismissive. The air in the room changes. It gets thick. Feels darker. I turn my face to see who spoke, and a form steps forward from the shadows.

How do you describe a human nightmare?

The pupils of his eyes are completely black. His face is not dirty but still seeps an evil that feels like I can taste it. I have read many books, learned of many villains, and this creature is definitely top shelf. I have known nothing of this kind of hate. He smiles and I have to physically shift to keep from peeing.

He turns and lets his horrible gaze rest on Nyx. "Well, this has turned out to be a fortunate turn of events, yes? You've proven quite elusive."

Nyx remains silent, glaring at him. He turns and motions with his hand, and two more awful Blighters emerge from the shadows. They twitch and writhe with disease and insanity, awaiting his word.

"Sweep the place. Then burn it to the ground," Black Pupils instructs, and the Blighters take off, searching the store.

NO! Jack and the boys, our books—this place! No, no, no! I want to shout a warning, look for them, but I know I can't. The Blighters may not know there are others here—I have to keep their attention.

One of the Blighters leans over the railing, giggling. He holds up our packs, all of our supplies, triumphant. My heart sinks.

Black Pupils calls out to the searching Blighters, "LARGE REWARDS for those that bring me others. UN-harmed."

Does he know how many we are? I hear the Blighters giggling and stomping from room to room. There are crashes and shouts. Just their presence here seems foul. I pray that the boys have gotten out.

"So you've been making some new friends, Nyx?"

She glares at him. Dead eyes. She is filled with hate for him.

He turns to me. It takes everything inside me to stare at him. I. Will. Not. Look. Away. "How many are in your group, little one?"

I summon everything in my dust-dry mouth and I spit at him. Missed his face but it runs down his collar. The spit runs slow motion down his front and… he smiles. He looks at my arm, bound behind my back. The

151

squatty Blighter behind me lifts my hands slightly so more of it is visible. Is he going to break it? I flinch but keep staring at him. He takes a black-gloved finger and runs it down my arm.

"LEAVE HER ALONE," Nyx shouts.

He smiles wider but doesn't take his eyes off my arm. What the NATCH is up with him and arms?

"Or what?" he croons, STILL with my arm.

"Take me. Just leave her. Let her go. You don't want her," Nyx says quickly. It's the first time I hear a tinge of fear in her voice.

"And why's that?" He looks back at my face, his dead eyes searching.

"She's… tainted. She has the Bleeds," Nyx spits out.

He turns and strides over to her. Fast. I try and think if I saw him take any steps. I feel woozy and kind of sick. "We'll see. Shadow will find out… but very noble, Nyx. Very."

SLAP!

He backhands her face so hard that she almost falls over. The tall Blighter behind her laughs and keeps her upright. I can see blood in her mouth.

But Nyx stands. She doesn't make a sound, and it makes me want to scream bad words in triumph. He raises his hand to strike again—and there is a loud THUD from upstairs. He spins around, searching. I look frantically around, hoping it's not one of the boys. *Jack, where are you?*

He calls up, "Rowan? Tenny? Check in!"

Running footsteps, giggling, then a disgusting patchy-haired Blighter leans over from the second floor. "Tenny in, boss. Tenny. Tenny. Tenny."

The Blighter waits, listening. Silence. And then—THWAP! He's hit in the neck.

A BLUE ROCK.

Jack!

Before anyone can do anything, the man is battered with a red rock, a green, blue—all rapid fire. He scrambles quickly for cover.

Let the war begin.

Chapter Thirty-Three
Mateo

One minute i'm licking cocoa dust from an old candy wrapper, an' the next there's screaming an' banging and everyone scatters. Jack goes one way, grabbing his slingshot, Logan and Digits another, so i just run straight. i look an' see a huge guy in a black coat an' a bunch of Blighters, an' they have Beckett and Nyx.

Nearly crap my pants.

i'm running down an aisle looking 4 something 2 fight with an' i'm just seeing all these plonker BOOKS. As i'm running, i see this busted, dirty Blighter flying down the aisle toward me. i duck in2 this room with MORE books an' i wait. He runs up, giggling and making weird noises with his mouth, and turns in2 the room an'—

BAM!

i NAIL him with a BOOK! i grabbed the biggest 1 i could see—something about World Geographs—an' crawled up on a shelf by the door. When that janked-out fool turned in, i got him good! i'm about 2 run out 2 tell the others when he moves, so i just sit on his head. I'm just sitting there trying 2 figure out what 2 do next when i hear someone coming—there's no giggly-weird noises so it isn't 1 of them, but i still freeze.

It's Jack. An' he's looking around all crazy.

"PSSST!" Guess i'm louder than i thought, cause he jumps and twists around. He sees me sittin' on this guy's head an' i smile.

"Is he dead?"

"Naw—just knocked out. Stood on this shelf and clobbered him with a book!"

"We need 2 tie him up or something—we gotta get the girls. Hurry!"

i get up an' start lookin' around. Books, books, books—LAMP! i grab it, yank out the cord, an' tie the Blighter's hands and feet in front of him, hog-style.

Jack is peeking out the doorway and pressurin' me 2 finish. "Someone's coming. Get ready."

i give the thumbs-up an' stand in the doorway. i can feel my legs shaking, so i shift from foot 2 foot. i can hear another Blighter guy snuffling and giggling just like the 1 i book-bonked. Can hear him coming right this way. Jack suddenly pulls me behind a bookcase. When the snuffly Blighter comes in the room, he sees his hogtied pal and runs right 2 him. When he does, Jack says "NOW!" an' we push that case RIGHT ON TOP of that dirty mucker. He shouts but it's cut off as he's either knocked out or dead.

Not sorry. i know damn well they are here 2 kill us. Maybe i'll feel bad later, but right now i wanna shout from the roof.

Jack and i check 2 see he's not moving an' then make a break 4 it.

As we're flying down the hall, i hear the black-coat goocher yell up, "Tenny!?"

There's no answer. Jack is flying toward a staircase across the floor. i'm right on his heels, trying 2 run an' look 4 Dige an' Logan. Not easy. But i'm going so fast cause i know we have an upper hand right now. Makes me feel like shouting again.

155

"Rowan?!" Black Coat shouts up. Nothing. We are almost 2 the staircase, then: "You leave me little choice. I will have 2 kill your friend. Come out now or she dies."

Beckett screams.

Jack skids 2 a stop. i jump 2 the side, just missing running him down. i finally stop an' see that Black Coat has a knife 2 Beckett's neck, an' i feel all the spit in my mouth dry up at once.   Jack runs 2 the railing. "STOP! WAIT!!"

i am frozen, staring at that knife an' Becks's tiny neck.

"AND?" Black Coat screams.

i jump up beside Jack, hoping he'll just take the damn knife down. He stares at us. it's maybe the scariest pair of eyes i've ever seen. i want 2 look away. Can't. i'm sure i would have farted if there had been any air in my body.

"Is that all of you?" He stares so hard.

Just then, i see Digits step out from behind a shelf 20 feet away and walk 2 the railing, his hands in the air like us. My heart aches a little. i'm supposed 2 protect him. i see him glance at me, an' he gives me this nod, right? And it seems so… *grown* that i feel my eyes sting. He's nodding at me that it's okay and i shouldn't feel bad. This somehow makes me feel all busted inside.

Dammit, Dige.

Black Coat still holds the damn knife 2 Becks, tho. She has tears running down her face an' is just staring at Jack, who stares at her an' Black Coat. i feel everything in me rise up so big with a need 2 kill this mucker.

156

Then he SMILES at us. "Good. Well, I'd like you 2 meet someone," he says, and be4 i can even look around, we're grabbed by a MONSTER.

Blackness.

Chapter Thirty-Four
Logan

It's chaos.

There's shouting, Beckett screams, and we all split in different directions. Once I see Digits is safe across the landing, he signals to me and I follow my own course. Jack and Mateo take out two of the Blighters, which I only hear instead of see because I'm crawling along on my belly. I can't see the man shouting from downstairs, but Digits signs that he's got Nyx and is holding a knife to Beckett's throat.

I want him to die.

I'm trying to position myself better when Jack and then Mateo give themselves up and stand at the railing of the second floor. Digits peeks his head out at me. I shake my head NO and sign, "Stay put," but then I see him look down.

And I know he won't listen.

Because—Beckett.

Digits stands and steps up next to Jack and Mateo.

It's up to me.

As his hands are in the air, Digits is signing to me the layout and positions of the Blighters, Nyx, and Becks downstairs. As his fingers fly, I try to place it in my head.

"Stage at twelve o'clock. Beckett and Black Coat at three o'clock. Knife to her neck. Nyx and tall Blighter at five o'clock, all face us. Watch for the rest—"

All of a sudden, a massive form appears behind them.

It scoops them up before I can move or anyone can fight. Mateo has time enough to scream, just before he passes out. The human wall carries them downstairs as if they're a couple of baby piglets and tosses them to the ground. I hear this more than see it.

And I'm on the move again.

I hit a corner and am able to look down from cover behind a couch. I see the Blighter in the black coat. He paces but seems to take no steps. I know he isn't floating but my mind keeps wanting to think he is. He paces as another Blighter ties everyone together. Digits looks up and finds me. He nudges Jack, who also scans and finds me. With his hands tied in front of him, Jack begins to lay out a plan, all the while never taking his eyes off the black coat and Nyx.

I watch Jack's hands spell out my next moves. I'm trying to focus, plot the layout, and absorb Jack's signing when—

"You look well… Daughter," Black Coat says to Nyx.

What the natch?

All I can think is "daughter of evil." And immediately I'm thankful that no one is in my head to hear it. Nyx turns red and looks right at Jack—dang it— and the gang, who all stare at her in shock.

"HE'S NOTHING TO ME!" Her voice cracks and I see her for the first time as a kid. Just like us. Scared. Angry. Just trying our best.

"Oh, come now. I wouldn't say that at all. Nyx and I are even closer than relatives. We have a unique and special symbiosis, don't we?"

159

I glance over and see him move toward Jack, talking to him. I stop, afraid, but Digits's hands sign, "NO. Keep going. Do. Not. Stop."

Brace up.

Gotta keep moving. I continue as I hear Black Coat say, "You see, I need her—quite literally. To survive. Well, to live—isn't that right?"

I can't afford to look but I know he's talking to Nyx. I can <u>feel</u> her silent hatred. It feels like it's burning through the floor underneath me. I keep crawling, and he keeps talking.

"See, my body has… betrayed me. And my daughter holds certain… attributes that enable me to thrive. Don't you, dear?"

There is nothing but silence. Everything in me wants to peek over and look but I cannot stop. I am all that stands between them and…

Survival.

"Your arms, Nyx," Jack whispers. "That's him, isn't it? Is he doing that to you?" I can hear pain in his voice. What's wrong with her arms?

I. Keep. Crawling.

"Oh, sweet, ridiculous boy. That body? Her fluids? They're not hers. She is merely a vessel. Her body has always been and now will always be mine. She was bred for it. You will see."

The words become a jumble. I can't make sense of what he says. I just need to plot my steps. Where I go. My actions. We can do this <u>if</u> I keep calm and—

"Call Shadow and the others—we will do it here," Black Coat says, and I hear the giant man stomp off. What others?! How many?! Have I lost my chance?

160

"This will go much smoother if you are silent," Black Coat says.

Moments later, Beckett screams, "JACK!"

I have to look. I peek out as that black-coated mucker squeezes the side of Jack's neck and—what?! Is he dead?! I'm about to stand when I see Digits's fingers wildly flashing. "NOT DEAD. PASSED OUT. Go, go, go. Keep going."

I slide back and keep going where I need to. I'm trying to just focus on the floor in front of me. Trying not to think about what I need to do. How they are all counting on me. My breath is coming so fast, I have to open my mouth so I don't start panting.

Terrified.

I glance down again and see the giant man, who Black Coat calls "Ash," move toward a huge hole in the front of the store. That's how they got in—it must've been the explosion we heard. Ash whistles out into the dark, and I see it.

A mass of Blighters: tall and short, dirty, giggling and screeching. They all swell forward, peering into the store, twitching and itching to get inside. Ash holds them off.

I crawl as fast as I can.

I hear movement. Tables and chairs scraping across the floor, Black Coat giving orders here and there. The giggling damn army of Blighters waiting and grumbling just outside.

Brace up.

I have to get things in order. I keep checking and double-checking, knowing that if I stop, if I look down again, I will just freeze and never move. It seems like hours, but I know it can't be.

I finally hear Black Coat say, "Let us begin."

I look. And I cover my mouth so I don't scream. Beckett, Dige, and Mateo are all tied in chairs, and there are tubes and stuff running from their arms into these clear bags on poles.

They are draining their blood.

Nyx is tied down on a table, a needle and tube in her arm as well, but it doesn't lead anywhere yet. I see a new guy—he's as white as a ghost, has no hair, and is fat and round. He looks like a human egg. He's sticking a needle into Jack's arm, who is now awake and looking around wild-like. He struggles. Black Coat says, "That's right, keep moving. A fuss will only increase the blood flow."

Then he steps out into the light.

I don't know if I make a noise, because all I hear is Beckett choke out a sob and Mateo half scream. Black Coat stands in the center of them, shirtless.

There are scabs and cuts and bruises all over his body. His joints are swollen and crooked like rotten apples. I can't see any skin that's not covered in some kind of sore. Some weep pus, others are fresh, some scarred over. He holds his hands out, showing them all.

"It's pitiful, no? I agree. Look on—this is my plight. My own blood does not clot. Even the tiniest of nicks can kill me. Get it, Nyx? That's irony for you. So… we replace it. I get regular purifying with fresh, healthy blood. Such as yours. I must thank you all now, as you won't be around for me to do so later."

He steps up to another table beside Nyx and lies down. "Of course, hers is the only blood I can accept without fear of rejection, sickness, or complication. Also, it has virtually CURED me of disease. So I keep her. Close. She is my living lifeblood and my answer to ultimate power."

The egg man steps up to him holding a needle, but he suddenly staggers like he's gonna faint or something. Black Coat jumps up and lifts Egg Man's shirt.

Oh, NATCH.

He's covered in dark black and blue bruises.

Black Coat lets out a HOWL. Like so crazy loud and filled with anger. I feel my legs start to shake. I've never heard anything like it. He grabs Egg Man's face. "How long?!"

Egg Man shakes his head and Black Coat turns to the giant and nods. The giant lifts Egg Man onto the table, and Black Coat jabs the needle into Egg Man's arm and hooks it up to Nyx's bag. Black Coat leans down to Egg Man, all angry-like. "You get just enough. The rest is mine. We will see if my theory stands. You better pray to any god you remember that it does."

I see Nyx's blood start to flow…

She has magic blood.

Black Coat waits, looking at the gang in their chairs. "We will drain you and then we will call in some of my citizens for… dinner. They have particular tastes."

I look where he nods and see them. Waiting. Drooling. Swaying. Ready to pounce on us. When Black Coat is done, they will enter.

And we are all dead.

I'm frozen. I have failed.

Tears start to blur my sight, but then I see Jack looking up. Straight at me. He looks at Digits then back at me. Digits finds me, and Jack starts signing with his free hand. Digits looks back and forth, reading. I read. I get it.

I'm moving again. I hear Jack speak up, covering my movements. "I'm… so sorry, Nyx."

I can't see her, but I think I hear her let out a sob. When something that doesn't cry cries, it hurts twice as deep. KEEP GOING, I tell myself.

Brace up.

"There are good people, Nyx. You can find them. You can be free. Just don't give up," Jack says, still loud enough to mask me. "I love you guys."

This time, I hear Becks cry out then say, "Jack. Ohh, Jack! I love you! I'm sorry for—I love you!" She starts sobbing. My heart is breaking but I can't stop. I need to get into position, but it will make noise. I need Jack to keep talking, I need—

Mateo to the rescue. "I'M SORRY I STOLE ALL YOUR JERKY, JACK. I STOLE IT IN THE TUNNELS—I ATE IT AND I DIDN'T SAVE ANY CUZ I WAS HUNGRY, AND I'M SORRY! I WISH I HADN'T, CAUSE IT WAS DRY, BUT MOSTLY I'M SORRY!" he wails. Perfect. I'm nearly there.

"SILENCE! SILENCE THEM, ASH!"

I peer out and see Ash walking toward Mateo with a bat. Mateo is screaming, and the Blighters outside start jumping around wildly at the noise, pressing to get in.

We are out of time.

164

Chapter Thirty-Five
Digits

Everything hangs in the balance.

I watch in slow motion as the one named Ash lumbers toward Mateo, bat raised high. I look back at Jack, then at Logan in his position. I hold out my free hand and sign as large as one small hand can:

ONE.

TWO.

THREE.

Logan descends from above, flying through the air. I watch his face. It is noble, determined, fierce.

My older brother, leaping to his possible death.

He lands on Mateo's giant cushion tower, rolls expertly, and tosses something behind the Blighters guarding the girls.

And the world explodes. Dust, pages, wood.

I realize that I'm the only one who doesn't wince at the sound. Again, time slows as I watch the silent action unfold. I look everywhere, seeking mouths to help me orient.

I watch Jack as he shouts to Logan, "The ENTRANCE!"

Logan climbs on top of a table, reaches into his pocket, lights another one of Badger's "toys," and throws it toward the entrance. As I watch its flight, I see the sea of Blighters surge forward.

Toward us.

The device explodes and I feel the vibration of it. Rubble and broken concrete rain down upon the advancing wave of Blighters. The monster Ash is now buried beneath a massive pile. I see it all. I am able to assess things differently, having not been hurt by the sound.

I watch as the dust settles and Logan runs to Jack, pulling the needle from his arm and cutting him free with his knife. As Logan removes my needle, Jack grabs the knife and runs to Beckett, removing her needle and cutting her free. He crosses to Mateo and frees him as well. He throws the knife to Logan, who catches it and cuts me free.

Another explosion.

I stand and turn wildly, seeking mouths to help me orient again. As the dust starts to settle again, I'm searching, searching. For her. I finally see her across the room, standing alone and yelling for Jack, who has gone for Nyx.

Suddenly, I see the one called Shadow stand up behind her. The blood on his face is the only color, the needle that delivered Nyx's blood still dangling from his arm. He raises a knife.

I cannot save her.

I cannot help her.

I am trapped by my silence.

I summon everything inside me and let loose with a scream—though Logan calls it my "Baby Eagle," it's the loudest sound I can emit.

Beckett's eyes look up at me. I point. There is no time. As she turns to meet her fate—

Mateo jumps in front of Shadow. He is screaming.

He pushes Beckett out of the way and points over Shadow's shoulder. "Hey! LOOK!"

A smile starts forming on my lips as I see what is coming.

Shadow glances to the side and Mats clasps his hands together and swings both fists as hard as he can at the side of the albino's head. He goes flying... and does not rise.

"KNOCK, YA PLONKER GHOST!"

I let out a "WHOOP" of triumph. *She is safe, she is safe, she is safe.* I think about what I signed to her when I thought we were about to die in that circle, the blood draining from us all.

I do not wish my confession back. I'm glad I told her.

I feel the ground shift. Another explosion? The vibration is not as strong. I watch where she's looking and see a giant fist come punching through a pile of rubble.

Ash is rising.

I make my way over the debris toward Mateo and Beckett. I see Jack jump over the table that Nyx was on. It has been tipped over in the chaos—I cannot see her. Jack disappears from view. I wait, scanning the room for the deformed one they call Xander. I know from his talk that he needs Nyx—he will not be far from her. Jack rises from behind the table, Nyx at his side. She is bloodied but all right.

"We need a way out!" he tells her, touching her hand. I smile in spite of everything happening.

"Follow me," she says and grabs his hand back.

Suddenly, Jack is ripped from her as Ash grabs him from behind and hoists him over his head like a sack of potatoes. I never saw him. Then he was there.

Nyx opens her mouth, screaming. I don't know what she says, but the fire and rage in her eyes are undeniable. She jumps on Ash's back, beating at him. It looks like when a fly lands on a horse, only to be swatted away with the swish of a tail. She slides off.

Jack is still suspended above the giant man's body. But Ash has shifted. He staggers. And I see it.

Nyx has plunged a needle into the beast's eye.

Blood gushes forth. He staggers, swinging his head wildly, and drops Jack to the ground, forgotten. He reaches for the needle, plucking it out.

Nyx turns her head to us. "RUNNNNN!!!"

Situation Report: Under siege.

Status: On the move.

Chapter Thirty-Six
Avery

She sits by the window, unmoving.

To break her vigil would somehow weaken Reese's journey. She wills him a strength she no longer has. Her breathing is labored, thick. It takes more effort each minute just to draw in the air. But still she remains, her eyes trained on the horizon.

Waiting.

Willa tries to help, with pillows and teas and gentle coaxing, but they don't talk much. Avery needs all her resolve to just sit there.

Watching.

Plus, the women know that if they give voice to their fears, they will never recover.

So Avery waits.

She watches.

She prays.

Time is running out. She is fighting for her life, just long enough... Just long enough...

To see her babies safe.

Xander

He rises from the explosion, bleeding freely from multiple nicks and cuts. His breathing is LABORED. He grabs Shadow's shirt. "The bag!"

Shadow, barely recovered, retrieves Nyx's discarded blood bag and dusts it off as he trots back to Xander. He produces a new tube and needle from inside his jacket and inserts it into the half-filled bag. Xander's knees buckle. He is panting. Shadow stands in front of him as Xander exposes his neck and largest vein. Shadow hesitates for a beat, looking at Xander, his master. Now vulnerable, small, compromised.

"Where will you go, Shadow? You will die without me. In seconds. DO. IT."

Shadow deftly plunges the needle into Xander's neck. Xander EXHALES as his body is almost instantly resurrected. As the blood pumps in. He watches as Ash quickly gives chase, blood streaming down his face.

And just as he has found her, he has lost her again.

He knows his time is limited. He saw this when he looked into Blue's eyes.

She will rally and she will fight for the girl. As her mother did so many years before…

He cannot risk losing Nyx. She is his. Genetically and by claim.

Xander's anger is only matched by his deep fear that he will not—that he <u>cannot</u> survive without her. He must find her and ensure that she will never leave him again. He will kill Blue as well—for her misguided and *intrusive maternal instincts. Unearned. She has no tie with the girl. He does.*

A deep guttural moan rises out of his throat as Xander bellows to his minions, "BRING THE GIRL TO ME—the rest are yours to take!"

Chapter Thirty-Seven
Jack

We're moving so fast it feels like we're flying up the stairs. Nyx leads and I bring up the rear. We are battered but alive.

Thanks to Nyx.

A needle to the eye seemed to only delay that monster. We're chased from all sides by rabid Blighters, the albino Shadow, and one-eyed Ash… who's understandably ready to kill us all.

I see Nyx's head look over the railing, panicked. "We have to go back down—there's no exit!" I can hear at least four Blighters just below us.

"CAN'T!" I scream, unable to say more. As we get to the top floor, I see Ash emerge across the balcony on the opposite stairs, blood streaming from his wound. He screams so loud, I'm sure even Digits flinches. We are all looking around for an escape…

And it hits me.

I grab Nyx's hand, pulling her to the railing that overlooks the main floor. I point three stories down. "JUMP!"

Nyx looks at me like I'm insane and pulls her hand away from me. I'm about to argue when I see a figure fly past me. Into space. Over the rail.

A red blur.

Figures that the mucker would take any opportunity for glory… or to be first. His form is clutch as he flies down through space and lands on Mateo's cushion mountain. I pull Nyx forward and we climb the rail as I see Ash just a few feet from Mateo.

"GOGOGO!" Mateo screams, pushing forward.

Beckett scrambles over and takes Nyx's hand. I take the other. Nyx is about to protest as—

We are flying. Before we know it, we land, intact. We scramble to try and untangle before—

Digits lands on my leg.

Mateo lands on... everything.

We're trying to squirm out from under him when he starts thrashing wildly. "NATCH!" he screams. "MOVE! THE JANKY MONSTER IS—" He shoves the entire pile of us aside just as Ash plummets from the sky and flattens all the cushions with a deep, ground-shaking THUD.

And lies still.

We stare at him, holding our breath.

Then we hear a low groan and I see a finger twitch and Ash starts to move.

Just then, Xander appears, recovered, and rips the needle from his neck. Shadow moves to place a bandage there but Xander KNOCKS his hand away. "GRAB THEM!" he screams to the horde of Blighters appearing through the dust and debris.

And we're moving again, right into the center of chaos. Rubble and grit everywhere, Blighters screeching and giggling and running amok. Nyx and I lead as we dodge them, running over toppled shelves, under tables, through legs—

Into a corner.

We're trapped. Five Blighters start to advance on us. I hold Nyx's hand and grab for Beckett's, pulling her behind me. Digits, Logan, and Mateo stand around us, facing them. We will fight. And we will lose.

But we will have lost together.

The Blighters close the distance. I can smell them. I can see their rotted mouths and dark, crazed eyes... They get closer and closer, descending upon us. All I can think about is my parents. I wish... I wish I could have helped my mom. I'm sorry I got Beckett involved in this. I couldn't... protect her. I couldn't protect any of us. The Blighters' chattering and mumbling is so loud I'm having trouble focusing. I grab for Beckett and Nyx, wanting just to hold them, hold everyone, when—

GUNSHOTS shatter the air. One. Then two more. The nearest Blighter flies backward, a chest wound already pumping blood. Another beside him is winged and spins, as a third looks around wildly, only to have his scabby knee shot out from under him.

As he goes down, I see the shooters.

It's Blue and Gentry. Behind them, a mass of Underfolk surge into the space, shooting, stabbing, and attacking.

"BLUE!" Nyx shouts.

Reloading, Blue shouts, "GET OUT, NYX! RUN!!"

A spray of blood spatters the side of my face. An Underfolk woman is swinging a bat at a Blighter's form on the ground. Nyx bolts, still hanging on to me and Beckett. We follow her to a rusted iron heating vent some twenty feet and two dead bodies away. Nyx plants her feet and yanks it up with a growl. She gestures, and Beckett, Digits, and Mateo dive into the blackness.

I look around for Logan.

WHERE IS LOGAN?!

174

I'm opening my mouth to shout for him when he races past me and disappears into the vent.

Nyx gestures for me to go, and I know there is no time to argue.

So I shove her down into the hole—they need her to lead them to safety. I look around, making sure we're not followed, and grab the grate cover to pull it on top of me as I drop my feet into the open space.

Then there's a movement in front of me and my hand is burning. Or freezing. I can't tell. Until I look.

Blood is spurting from it, and I see someone's fingers on the ground.

Mine.

Three fingers lie on the ground.

Then the pain hits and I want to throw up but I can't breathe.

I look up and see Xander. A machete in his hand and a smile of infinite evil on his face. I watch with a kind of distance as my blood drips slowly from the knife to the ground.

I feel something tug on the back of my shirt.

Blackness.

The rest is in flashes. Like Dad's old viewfinder that shifts pictures in front of eyeglasses.

Torchlights weave in the blackness.

I am floating.

My hand is on fire.

Black.

Nyx's face.

Above me. She's wavy. Like she's behind a screen of heat. My arm is moved, but it just feels like ice.

"Tighter! You have to wrap it tighter! I NEED LIGHT!… Jack?! Jack can you—"

Black.

I'm bouncing.

Something on my stomach.

Hard to breathe.

Torchlight beams move everywhere.

I am bouncing. On someone's shoulders.

Black.

Beckett. Sniffling and crying as she sings, "*Great big house in New Orleans… Forty stories hi-igh… And every room that I've been in, filled with chicken pie.*"

I turn my head to find her.

"Jack! I'm right here! Mats has you. Just hang on, okay! Just—"

Logan screams from somewhere behind us, "THEY'RE COMING! MOVE IT."

Black.

Harder bouncing, and my entire arm is on fire.

A glow of flames somewhere behind us.

I wonder if I'm dying.

A loud EXPLOSION propels us forward in a lurch.

Black.

Bouncing.

Gunshots.

I want to vomit.

Black.

Then brightness. Daylight? I want to go back to sleep. Hard to talk. I hear shouts and voices in the distance.

Can't focus.

I'm laid down. The ground is hard. Cold. Fog. Everywhere.

Logan, his shouts piercing the fog that wants to take me. "We're still in the CITY?! DAMMIT, we're right by the store!"

Which store? Why is it so bright?

Nyx shouts back at him, her anger only slightly louder than her fear. "Somebody's BOMBS shut off all our exits."

I want to ask what day it is.

Beckett fills my line of vision. "Jack?" she says gently.

I start to blink and look around. We're on a city street. Still in Blighter territory. I smell smoke. Hear fighting and screams. I have to get up. So heavy.

"Beckett?" Nyx's voice, but it sounds so small. She's scared.

I use all the energy left in me to lift my head. And I see.

Nyx stands off to the side of the street.

Ash stands behind her. His hands encircling her throat.

He wears no expression. Simply stands, blood drying down his massive face, and he begins to choke the life from her. Mateo, Logan, and Digits jump up and stand, defensive. Ready. Beckett stands in front of me, shaking.

I will my body to move. I can only roll to the side.

The pain hits. My hand lights on fire again. Stars fill my vision, and the black wants to take me again. I blink. Once, twice.

Just trying to see HER.

My body is moving. I sit up, never taking my eyes from her.

I pull a leg under me, using my good hand to steady myself. I swallow the sick that threatens to come up.

Staring at her. Her face grows red but she is focused. Alert.

Staring right back at me.

This pulls me to stand. I feel Beckett put a hand on my arm, trying to pull me back.

I shake her off and take a step forward.

Ash. Blank, soulless.

Nyx. So sad. Resigned. Leaving me. Two more steps. So… close.

Ash hoists Nyx onto his shoulder as if she were a grain sack. He starts to walk away. She twists her head up and looks at me. "Just RUN! He only wants me—get Jack out and—"

"Nyx! NO!" I hear someone yell. It's me. I reach out my good hand to her. My movement disconnected. More falling forward than walking.

She reaches her hand out.

We connect. A charge. A shock between us. I try to hold but the colossus propels forward.

Then stops.

He just stops. Doesn't turn or shake or move.

Then he is on his knees, falling so hard I want to see if the old pavement has cracked. But I don't.

I only look at Nyx. Her eyes widen in shock. No more aware of anything happening than I am, but unwilling to look away from me. In slow motion, he drops her to his side. I hold on. She falls and scrambles up beside me as Ash thuds to the side.

And I see him.

"Dad?" I croak. Sure that I am dreaming.

My father looks up and lets out a sob of relief, letting go of a knife stuck hilt-deep in Ash's neck, his red blood pooling from him and running into the cracks of the street.

My legs give out.

My father.

He catches me, lowers me to the street, my body resting on his lap. He sobs again, cradling my bandaged hand gently. I blink and see Beckett, crying, hugging him from behind. Then I hear Mateo.

"DAD!!" And I see Uncle Garrett. Logan and Digits crowd in, everyone hugging everyone.

Where's Nyx? I lift my head. She's standing off to the side. Awkward. Lonely. Doubtful. I want to bring her into the hug. I want to tell her it's safe.

I want her to know love. Ours. Mine.

It's Beckett—the dog tamer, the animal lover, slayer of cans, coyotes, and horse turds—who bridges the gap. She reaches out a hand to Nyx, who steps forward, timid but hopeful.

"This is Nyx. She's with us," Beckett states plainly.

I can feel myself smile. I swat away the tear that drips down my cheek before she can see it. Then, in his plain, perfect way, I hear my dad say, "Nice to meet you, Nyx. Welcome aboard. You happen to know the quickest way out of here?"

I see Nyx look up at him shyly. Then that corner of her mouth twitches.

The smile.

Chapter Thirty-Eight
Beckett

We follow Nyx.

It's scary and it's hard, but we're together. Dad and Uncle Garrett are bloodied and bruised, and they don't talk much about what they went through to find us. As we race from the city, I keep trying to ask them what happened... until Jack tells me to stop.

I do.

Not because Jack is bossing me around but because I'm happy. We're taking Nyx HOME. I keep trying to tell her stuff about the farm and our lives. She listens but won't give much. I leave it alone after a while. I know not to push.

It seems like the longest journey in the world. After I decide to be quiet, I just keep thinking about how it is taking SO LONG for us to get back home. To get back to Boo and the pigs and SHOWERS and my bed.

And my mom.

Dad said she was "doing okay" when he left, but he has "the face." That face that he gets where his jaw gets all hard and he doesn't offer details.

That means it's bad.

This is the longest journey in the world. So. Long.

At one point, when I'm aching so hard to go faster, Digits reaches out and squeezes my hand. I look back at him and he nods. All serious. I feel like that nod says, "Just hold on. It will be okay."

Just the one nod.

Seems like it helped get me through. I don't really know what it meant, could have been a dang twitch for all I know, but I chose to take it how I needed to take it.

We cross past the Wall, and all I want to do is run. All these people are there, waiting to meet us. Our people. The guards and Mr. Benton, who's kinda like the mayor, and all our friends. They have water and jerky and fresh horses. We grab what we can and mount up. Nyx rides with Jack, cause she doesn't know from riding... yet.

And we race. As hard as the horses will take us. And after going so slow for so long, it feels wonderful to gallop across hills and roads toward home.

As we fly down the last stretch of road to our farm, I see Aunt Willa standing on the porch, shielding the sun from her eyes. As soon as she catches sight of us, she starts running down the road.

Never seen Mateo move so fast or cry so hard as when he flew off that horse and into her arms. Willa is crying just as hard as she picks him up, which is no small deal. "Oh, thank god! Oh, my sweet child!" she sobs, spinning him.

Jack and I run up to her. I have a lump in my throat and can't talk. Jack squeaks out, "Mom?"

And Aunt Willa looks DOWN. I think she inhaled to say something, but Jack and I both just run for the house.

WHY DID SHE LOOK DOWN?

I burst into the house, Jack right beside me. I'm trying my best not to start crying. BRACE UP!

"MOM?! MOM!!"

I run into the living room, where she's taken to staying. I look to the couch, and her blankets are there but they're all folded up. The table is covered in Willa's medicines and broths.

No Mom.

"Jack—" I breathe, and he spins fiercely and says, "NO. Don't."

So I bite my lip. I bite it so hard I can taste blood. My mind starts whirling. Mom in the kitchen. Mom laughing. Mom singing me songs. Mom, Mom, Mom—

"Babies?"

I turn and I see HER! She's standing in the doorway. She's skinnier, looks worse, but dammit, she's standing and breathing and alive.

Jack and I rush up to her and help her to the couch, and I don't even care if her wrists feel so thin or that her breath is ragged. I hug her and kiss her and cry.

I cry out loud and long, and I don't give a damn.

Jack cries too. And we sit there, crying and holding her and letting her pet us and hold us back. She sees Jack's bandaged hand and lets out a yelp of pain and sorrow. Just that quickly, Willa is there, tending to it. My dad comes in and leans down and kisses my mom. He glances over at Willa and sees Jack's hand and the missing fingers.

He and my mom both make sounds I've never heard. My mom grabs my dad and starts crying harder. He sits real fast next to her, like he's gonna pass out. Willa just keeps working. Jack won't look at his hand. He turns to look at our parents. There's sweat beading up on his forehead and he's a little pale, but he puts on this smile to them.

"It's okay, Mom. You guys, it's okay. I'm here…
most of me anyway."

And that smile again, through his hurt, and I
wanna hug him so hard, but I can't cause Willa is
working on him. He keeps the brave face. Mom just
keeps nodding and Dad looks like he wants to burn down
the world, but Jack—he smiles that smile at them until
they calm… just a bit.

I see the others trickle in, but it's through tears
that don't seem to want to stop. My dad starts nodding
"okay" at Jack and just keeps rocking my mom, who is
also nodding, tears still falling. They look at each other
and nod. And smile. And cry.

I cry harder.

I wipe my face and see that the boys have already
grabbed fistfuls of Willa's food and are devouring it.
Nyx stands in the shadows.

That won't do.

I take my mom's hand and say, "Mom, this is
Nyx. She's going to stay here, okay? But no chores for
her for the first month—we don't wanna run her off."

My mom looks up at Nyx, collecting herself and
working her magic. She can tame any animal and put any
human at ease. She's incapable of lying with her feelings
or her heart. It just shines through no matter what she
does or says. She lets loose with one of her best smiles.
The one that says, "Welcome. You are safe." I see Nyx
smile back. It's one of her small, reluctant smiles, but for
Nyx, this means everything.

"Nyx. That's a beautiful name. It suits you,"
Mom says simply, still smiling. Nyx blushes a little and
nods. It's good.

Willa rebandages Jack's hand, and though I've seen all manner of injury on this farm, I cannot watch. I can't see what that evil goocher has done to him. He turns to Mom. He's all serious. He's about to cry.

"Mom… the books… They were in the store and there was the fight and…" He swallows real fast. Choking on it. My heart wants to break right out of my chest for him.

Mom reaches out with her tiny arm and brushes his hair. "Shhhh, shhh, my sweet boy… All I ever need is you guys. It's the best medicine." I wish this were true. I wish it with all my body. But I'm looking at her. I see.

Jack pulls away from her touch, upset. "But I had them, Mom—there were so many—everything—everything. Dad, we have to go back." He's getting wild-eyed and Dad steps up, trying to calm him. I stand up too, ready to turn right around and fight the world beside him. This cannot be how it ends.

"Uhhh, Jack?" Logan speaks up over our growing frenzy. I turn and look at him, an insult on my lips cause I know he's gonna try and make this about HIM and—

He's holding up a huge book. It's a medical text.

I bite back my insult as Jack's face brightens with surprise and hope.

"I grabbed your pack before we left," Logan says. Wow. He's all… humble? It's real. I try and burn this into my brain for the next time he makes me so angry I wanna throttle him. Jack rushes over and looks at the book, then at Logan. They have a weird, silent "boy conversation," give each other an awkward but real "boy hug," and Jack takes the book to Willa. She starts paging

185

through it as we all look on. Except my mom. She just holds and strokes us.

I hear Digits cough and I look up, knowing that a Digits cough means something. Usually something mind-bending and important.

He is also holding a medical book. Jack crosses to him and, teary, signs, "Thank you." And takes it. I'm smiling as Digits holds out another book. Only this time, he's holding it toward me.

To Kill a Mockingbird.

It's the one I was reading in the bookstore. The one that was so beautiful, I could barely read it. The one whose pages smelled of truth and knowledge.

He got it. For me.

I look at it, then at him, tears falling, and without thinking, I sign, "Me too." Because I feel it. I know it. What he told me in that bookstore, his confession that he signed to me across the room… I felt it then.

And I feel it now.

I guess he wasn't expecting that, though, cause he just stares at me, his mouth hanging all open and shocked-looking. I let out a laugh and don't care who's looking funny at me.

Jack is hovering over Willa as she pages quickly through the books. I can feel my dad staring at her too. And my mom NOT staring.

"Are they… enough?"

Willa looks up and I see it. Disappointment. It's quick and she tries to cover it. "Well… it's a start. We can…"

We have failed.

Chapter Thirty-Nine
Mateo

My mouth is so full of Mom's pie, i can't say it right, so i just spit out what i can. "Anti-co… ca… cacagens— The SYMBOL!" i spew crumbs an' stuff all over, but i gotta get it out. i reach down in2 my pants—can't believe i 4got about that goocher thing i had 2 keep down there, but… pie.

Everyone's staring at me, an' i keep spitting out pie and talking. "See—I knew the one symbol that you had in all your books, Mom. The star and stuff. I saw this but then that goofy toothless bastard started chasing me an' i shoved it in my drawers, an' it was hell 2 land on when i did that last couch dive… Sorry, hold on—"

i see 'em all still lookin' at me an' it's taking 4ever. Finally, i whip it on outta there an' hold that damn thing up. It has THE SYMBOL. The one from all my mom's books. The one she's been lookin' at when she's been trying so hard 2 fix all the folks with the Bleeds.

Like Jack's mom.

This SYMBOL is all huge, and i just know it's all about them anti-cacagens or whatever.

My mom rushes up an' starts paging thru it.

Everyone's all quiet. Feels like no one's breathing.

But i see my mom's eyes. They're all bright and sparkly as they fly over the words. So i'm smiling be4 she even says it. "Oh, sweet boy—I KNEW you could listen. This might be what I need." An' she's all teary an' bright. She looks at Jack, who's staring so hard an' hopeful at her, i can feel it. She nods at him. i see tears start 2 fall outta her face.

But it's happy tears.

Jack runs up 2 me and grabs me in the biggest hug ever. "Thank you and your giant underwear, Mats! HERO!" He's laughing. i hug him back real hard an' lift him up. i dunno why but i kinda start crying.

Happy tears.

Chapter Forty
Logan

It seems so normal now.

I mean, one minute we were in the middle of a war with Blighters and now we're here. On Jack's porch. Mateo and I are poking a big beetle with a stick, trying to herd him. Digits is reading, Beckett is playing with her dog, and Jack is pointing out stuff on the farm to Nyx. It's just so… <u>normal</u>. I mean, Mateo's mom is hard at work fixing up some medicines for Jack's mom, Jack's and Mateo's dads are getting ready to ride out, and everyone is calm, cleaned up, and fed.

It took a lot to get Beckett and Jack to leave her side. But no one really argues with Miss Willa… or at least they don't win. It was pretty scary seeing Jack's mom, though. She looked… bad. But Miss Willa is so happy with the books. She and Jack's mom both seem… lighter, I guess.

We did that.

About as swank as it gets.

Did it all even happen?

I mean, I feel good—like clutch. We faced an <u>army</u> and <u>won</u>. We left our town, traveled to the city, and really did it. It kind of feels like it happened to another person. But it was us. I feel a kind of weird sadness, I guess. I can't really place it. Just a strange feeling.

It's going to be hard to go back to <u>normal</u> after doing what we did and seeing what we saw.

Jack's dad walks out, ready to go. He has a gun. "Need to pick up some more supplies from Willa's for

Mom. Garrett will go there while I talk to the guys at the Wall. Might be a long night."

"I'll get Mercy for you," Becks says, and she runs around the side of the house.

"You think they're coming here?" Jack asks what everyone is thinking.

"I don't really… not after the maze Nyx led us out through." He gives Nyx a wink, which makes her smile a little and blush. "But it's good just to be sure for a while," he says, looking at Jack like he's grown. It's funny how, in just a few days, I've seen how they talk to each other. Nothing obvious, just different. Like they have a new understanding or something. I guess fighting death can do that. I start thinking about my pa and how we don't talk much. I wonder if he'll talk differently to me now that I've done what I did.

Mateo's dad comes out of the house, and he and Mr. Weller are about to go when Beckett calls out from the barn. Her voice sounds… wrong.

I look up—and my breath leaves me.

"Dad?" Beckett's voice is so small. Nothing like the Beckett I know. She comes around the corner. Shadow stands just behind her, holding a needle to her throat. He wears no expression. I can see Beckett's legs shaking as she tries her best not to move.

There is no time. Digits is up. Ready. Jack, Nyx, Mateo and I are up. Ready.

Mr. Weller goes very still and takes a step toward her.

Suddenly, Xander steps out from behind them. He's so calm. Cold.

"Ah-ah-ah. I wouldn't. Shadow will press that plunger and embolize her with one tiny bubble of air," he sneers as Mateo's dad places a hand on Mr. Weller's arm. Trying to calm him.

We can take them. It's just the two of them. We can do it. I get that feeling in my gut. I'm ready.

Mr. Weller holds up his hands. "You're outnumbered. Let her go, and we will let you leave." His tone is low but... kind of scary.

I'm ready.

Xander just smiles. Something in my gut clenches, thinking that it will just grow and spread across his face until it splits in two. He glances at Shadow, who lets loose with a high whistle.

Blighters.

They step out of shadows and from behind the barn and the pasture. They keep coming. It's maybe twenty or so. I'm shaking too hard to count. They all slink up behind Xander and stand, swaying and giggling. They are all so plonking crazy it hurts to look at 'em.

They are ready.

Xander never takes his eyes off Mr. Weller. "What were you saying about those numbers?"

"What do you want?" Mr. Weller keeps his hands up.

Xander whips his black-eyed face toward Nyx. It's like a knife, that look. I have an urge to step in front of her.

Jack is already there. Of course.

"Her. That is all. Give her to me, and I will give your spawn back."

"No. Dad. No." Jack's tone is low like his dad's. Firm. Grown.

Mr. Weller cracks a little. He looks from Beckett to Nyx and back to Xander. He's not panicking but... he's a dad. He tries again. "Let's work something out. I'm sure we could trade plenty of food and water. I don't know your need for the girl, but—"

Xander interrupts him. "You see that pale fellow with the needle? He was set for death only hours ago. See now? That is because of her. Her lifeblood saved him. It will save anyone I deem it to—including any of your sick. So give her to me. We will leave you some blood and we will walk away. You will live and never see us again."

"NO." Jack's voice is loud and strange-sounding. He's holding his dad's shotgun in the crook of his hurt arm, his good hand on the trigger. He slowly lifts it.

And levels it at Xander.

Xander smiles. Amused. "Really, boy? And what do you hope to accomplish, even if you could get a shot off? Your sister will die at your hand."

If it's possible to suffocate from hate, I might be doing so now.

Jack just stares at him for a couple seconds, but his face... I've known him all my life. He's my best friend in the world... and I've never seen a look like that on him. It's blank but... fierce. It's all in his eyes.

I'm ready.

Jack slowly turns and holds the gun... on Nyx. What the NATCH?!

I hear Xander suck a breath in—scared. The Blighters behind him whine and growl, getting all worked up. Xander is fighting to stay calm. I can hear the scared right underneath.

Jack speaks, his eyes never leaving Nyx's face. That weird <u>thing</u> is sparking off all around them. She stares right back at him.

"I have two shots. First is for your lifeline—her," he says, and Nyx steps up to the barrel—ready! They are just staring at each other.

I hear Beckett whine from under Shadow's deadly white hand.

"The next is for you. See, I figure all I have to do is graze you, right?" Jack stares him down.

"Then you and your family will be torn to shreds."

"But you? You will be dust," Jack says, then he turns to look back at Nyx. She has tears in her eyes that she won't let fall. She nods, steps up to the gun, and places the end of the barrel on her heart. She nods again at Jack and the tears finally fall.

He just stares at her, blank.

Xander takes a step forward, hands out. "NO! EVERYONE WILL DIE! IT WILL BE FOR NOTHING!" He is frozen. The Blighters behind him groan and chomp their teeth.

Jack is just staring at Nyx. "Did I ever tell you what my favorite color is?"

SPANK THIS, he's gone craz—

"Well, I HOPE it's BLUE." Nyx smiles. Why is she smiling? I follow Nyx's eyes...

Blue comes out from behind the other side of the house, Gentry and Dolly right next to her. We stand between them and Xander and his Blighters.

Xander lets out a bark of a laugh. "And what are YOU going to do, mole woman?"

"Some cleaning up." She makes a weird clicking with her tongue and slowly, one by one, UNDERFOLK step forward from the other side of the farm. They are all armed. There are more of them than Blighters, but not many. Still, the numbers have changed. They stand behind Blue.

Ready.

"You'd sacrifice all your people for them?" Xander shouts to her.

"I don't have to. All we have to do is get YOU, Xander. We cut off the head and the snake dies—and all YOU need is one tiny little cut, ain't that right?" And she smiles at him. It is beautiful and scary all at once.

Xander turns and calls to Nyx. "You will never outrun your destiny. The world now knows your secret and they will rip you apart to live longer. You will never be free."

I see Jack look at her and wink. She smiles even though she has a gun at her heart. Jack turns and moves the gun back to Xander and says, "She's already free."

I'm about to jump—I can't take it anymore— when suddenly a GREEN ROCK dings right into Shadow's face.

It all goes in slow motion.

I turn and see Digits. How did he get up on the roof!? He was just right beside me! He's standing tall and holding up his slingshot.

Shadow ducks, holding his bloody face, and Beckett ducks and rolls away, out of sight.

Xander brings a gloved hand down and the Blighters all surge forward, screaming and swinging.

The Underfolk storm forward to meet them.

We are stuck in the middle.

But I. Am. Ready.

Jack calls and we all climb up the hitching post to the porch cover and then the roof, like we've done a million times before. Digits is there with all our slingshots and ammo ready. I will hug him later for this.

We fire into the crowd, being sure to hit only the Blighters. We cannot find Xander or Shadow in all the mess, but I see Blue, Dolly, and Gentry leading a charge toward where they were. Jack has his dad's gun and rushes to the edge of the roof. Nyx points, and we see a fat, bloody Blighter about to jump Mr. Weller from behind. Jack fires and takes out his leg. Nyx is there with the gun's ammo, helping him reload. Mateo fires wildly, screaming, "It's ON NOW, YA JANKY, FILTHY FREAKS!" And he points down the road.

It's pretty much all of Lander's End, riding in on horses and moto-bikes. All armed. All flying full tilt.

We are ready.

Chapter Forty-One
Digits

Reinforcements have arrived.

Our team remains intact with only minor injuries. We have made a stand on the roof and are prepared to do whatever necessary. The enemy must be eliminated—but I can only think of her.

When I saw Beckett on the end of that needle, I felt my body moving before my mind.

One of the advantages of being deaf is that sometimes people forget about you. There is a point where some become tired of showing their mouths for me to read, do not sign, and just… choose to forget that I'm around.

I have experienced this only on rare occasions because I was born and grew up in the same township with the same people. They are all used to and comfortable with me.

But strangers, such as the Blighters and the Underfolk, are awkward with the difference and therefore sometimes choose to forgo adapting. I have learned to take advantage of these occasions.

I hide in plain sight.

This is how, in the middle of a standoff, I was able to duck into the house, warn Willa and Avery, retrieve weapons and ammo, and secure a position on the roof. Out of sight.

The hardest part was watching and steeling myself not to just attack as soon as I was up there.

To watch Beckett, at the will of that animal, Shadow… to see her so helpless and afraid.

I felt the rage in my bones. But I held fast, knowing that a hasty attack could kill her. I lay there, reading their back-and-forth and feeling my entire body shake with a suppressed need to act.

To rescue.

Finally, I did act, and it was executed well and effectively. She scrambled to safety before the horde descended. I will not see her harmed again. One would have to kill me to do so.

Here we are on the roof, watching a war unfold fifteen feet below. I pace and scan every corner, watching for her. I know her. She will not stay hidden for long.

The army of Landers is led by Mr. Benton, who must have rallied everyone on his way here from the Wall. As I try to scan the faces, I see nearly everyone I know. Men, women, some teens.

Even Badger has come out to… "help." He is throwing his devices into groups of Blighters, sometimes effectively, sometimes not so much. After the first couple, he starts using his blacksmith hammer. Much more effective. The Landers seem to be aware that the Underfolk are "friendlies," and they fight side by side.

It's a brutal, beautiful dance.

Benton gallops his horse straight into a group of five Blighters converging on an Underfolk woman— Mel, our original captor. He swings a club from side to side on his mount, and Blighters fall in his wake like filthy dominoes. Mel stands to fight on with a nod between them.

The McNulty brothers jump from their horses and tackle two Blighters who are beating Mr. Walscot.

They pummel them, help the older man up, and form a triangle of swinging fists.

Blue kicks out the legs of a Blighter from behind and Jack's dad appears out of nowhere with a fencepost, knocking him out.

Garrett is stabbed in the side by a tall, twitchy Blighter who stands over him, holding the gore-covered knife, about to finish the job. Suddenly, an arrow pierces his throat. Behind it is Dolly, the Underfolk woman. She runs forward, Garrett gets the knife, and they fight their way to the edge of the mass.

And here we are, high and relentless.

Logan and Mateo stand at the roof's edge, firing rock after rock as precisely as they can.

Logan is in his element. Mateo is making his talents useful by yelling at the Blighters nearby. Once they're distracted and looking toward him, Logan or I will fire.

It'd almost be comical. If people weren't dying.

Jack and Nyx cover the other side of the battle. They are a finely tuned machine. One will fire the gun while the other uses a slingshot or spots targets. Then one reloads, and they trade. It's like two separate bodies functioning as one.

It's inspiring.

I'm desperate to know where Beckett is. I am about to jump down and go search for her when I SEE HER!

She's sprinting toward us, dodging expertly in and out of fighting. She looks up and we lock eyes briefly. I have to go to her. I move toward the edge of the roof—and I see her fall.   A toothless female

Blighter has grabbed her ankle. The beast stands over her, cackling and spewing spit. The Blighter is about to tear her apart when I fire at her square in the forehead.

She goes down. Beckett scrambles up and grabs my rock.

She looks up at me.

I stand as tall as I can, brace my stance, and:

Three fingers of one hand encircle three fingers of the other hand.

Then I hold up four fingers.

I point at her.

"The world for you."

She blushes and smiles, signing back. She now knows my heart and has returned my greatest hope with a simple "me too." She knows. She reciprocates.

I could exist a thousand lifetimes in that moment. But her smile suddenly fades and time slows even further. I am lifted violently upward. I catch a glimpse of dirty, matted hair and smell…

Blighter.

I hear Beckett scream. I have no time. I am going off this roof. I am dangling over the edge.

Look away, Beckett.

Suddenly, I'm yanked backward, away from the edge, out of the air, and back down to the rooftop. I see the Blighter thrown back and fall out of sight as I land. I lose sight of him just as I realize I'm rolling. I'm going over. I grab the edge of the roof, but it's slippery and I'm weak.

And there he is. Logan. The one who saved me moments ago, and hundreds upon hundreds of times before. He grabs my wrist, and it's as if just his touch is a blanket all around me. I look up into his eyes.

That grin. That hair. My brother.

Before I can smile back, a Blighter stands behind him.

I have no words to save him. I try and I am too late, too silent, too deaf.

The Blighter twists his neck and I feel all the bones. I feel the end of my hero. I feel the sound of my life changing forever. I SCREAM. I don't know if it makes a sound.

His body falls past me and lands on the ground. I hear the thud. I drop. I don't care if my legs break.

They don't. I turn and run to his lifeless body, weeping and crying. No air. I see Jack screaming and running toward us as he raises his father's gun and shoots the Blighter off the roof. I'm aware of a body falling somewhere behind us.

I feel Beckett's arms around me. Everyone is crying. There's chaos. I see the Blighters behind them start to retreat and run away, our people chasing them off, but it means nothing.

He is gone.

Logan is gone.

Chapter Forty-Two
Jack

The aftermath.

We watch from the roof just outside my room. It's dark now and we're all quiet. It's exhaustion. It's shock. It's a grief so deep it closes our throats. Nyx, Beckett, and I are sitting as close as possible. Mats is crammed in the corner. Snoring. He fought a hero's battle and has earned it. His sleep is no reflection of his feelings, just how he processes. I'm jealous. Each one of us is caught in our own memories of what we just went through.

It was an impossible journey. Made by "kids." Through uncharted, treacherous territory. Facing the unknown. Standing together. Fighting.

For a book.

It seems impossible that it even happened. But I feel the absence of my best friend and an ache in his place, and I know that it did. We watch the cleanup of our pasture and field, marred by bodies that will never move.

Some ours.

More theirs.

I would say we "won," but friends have fallen. Given their lives in a battle they never foresaw.

For a book.

I see Beckett watch as Digits and his parents leave in a wagon. Digits looks up at Beckett. He has vengeance in his eyes as they turn for home, Logan under a sheet in the wagon. He's different. Something I've never seen before looks out from behind those eyes.

Beckett lets out a SOB as a fresh wave of grief hits. Nyx puts an arm around her. I put an arm around both of them, wanting to erase it all… for all of us. Wanting to return Beckett's innocence. Digits's hope. Logan's grin and crazy-making competitiveness. Wanting to fix Nyx, to make up for the injustice that she has endured. Wanting her to tell me what's in her head… her heart. Wanting to brush back that stray hair and see her green eyes.

But I cannot.

So I just hold on.

We must have fallen asleep like that because it seems the fires lighting the field are different when my dad pokes his head through the window. "Nyx, I set up a cot for you in the kids' room—figured y'all may want to stay together?"

We all nod, consenting without conference.

Beckett sniffles and asks, "How's Mom?"

Our dad's expression isn't what we want to see. "Willa is having… trouble breaking through. The books are… amazing, but we're running out of—"

I'm so angry, I can't stop the tears, and I blurt, "It was all for nothing—"

Beckett won't have it. "No! No, Jack—don't say that! We BEAT them. We found Nyx, we got the RIGHT books—" She jumps up, already ahead of the argument. "Dad! We can go back! We can—"

I feel the cold against my side as Nyx suddenly stands, facing my dad. "Can you take me to her? We'll… we'll probably need Willa too."

It feels like Becks and I are holding our breath. Because we know what this means.

I am praying my dad doesn't start arguing or asking questions. She might change her mind. *Please, Dad...*

He looks at Beckett and me. I don't know what he sees, but he looks back at Nyx for a moment, then... just nods. She follows him silently into the house.

I think we're afraid to move. Beckett grabs my hand and we lean on each other. It's weird to think that this simple, pure gesture would have been unheard of between us just a week ago.

"Jack? You think it's gonna work? Her blood?"

"Yes. I do."

I feel her exhale. "Yeah."

We sit there like that for a while and let the tears fall as the journey, the cost, the pain, and the joy all collide upon us.

For this moment, though, there is hope.

A mockingbird perches on the edge of the Last Bookstore. It takes off, flying through the city and the surrounding forest. Past the burning fires and distant fighting. It lands on a hilltop near two figures. Battered, but not broken. One wears a familiar pair of boots, their laces covered in teeth. Next to the man in the black trench coat is an abnormally large one-eyed coyote, who lays his head down beside his new master, watchful but tame.

They are silent as they gaze toward the distant smoke from the chimney of the Weller farm.

Once, not too long ago, he entered the city alone... and he conquered.

He hums his familiar tune and plans for his coming resurrection.

THANK-YOUS:

Thank you to Michelle and Jane, Michael, and especially Jed, who believed in this before the rest of the world did. Thank you to Elizabeth, Troy and Damien McNeely. Thank you to Bri for the gorgeous cover, to Mollie for doing such a great job editing and to Jhennifer and Metamorfic for enabling this to get out into the world!

Brooke's Thank-Yous

Thank you to my mom, Chloe, who never gave me any limits or boundaries to what I could be or do and gave me unconditional love throughout. To my dad, Bert, who told me he was proud of me even when I couldn't hear it. Thank you to the love of my life, Doug Purdy, who got up early, stayed up late, and did a thousand pickups and drop-offs and weird school lunches in between so I could sit at a computer and create worlds. Who always, always, always makes me laugh and makes me realize how I chose so well. To my kids, Max and Scout, for inspiring this book and reading everything I do and being two of the most amazing humans to ever grace this marble. To my VILLAGE at bootcamp, who have kept me outta jail just by showing up and listening, sharing and making me laugh. To my righteous women: Jenica, Colette, Joelene, Briana, and Jen—you lift me in more ways than I can even count.

And thank you to anyone who has ever told me "no." Or "you can't." Vengeance is a powerful motivator. Not as good as love, but it can fuel some pretty creative results. So, thanks. And suck it.

Colette's Thank-Yous

Thank you to the KIDS, the amazing group of creative, brave, smart, and unique KIDS who enrich my life and inspired this book. Thank you, Zac, Dylan, Max, Scout, Augie, Channing, Lyle, Harrison, Adelaide, Malcolm, Elan, Ari, Carina, Madison, Morgan, Jonathan, Emory, August, Skye, Oona, Stella, Sadie, Olivia, Matthew, Noah, Leila, Bodhi, Fifer, Jocelyn, Liam, Finn, Zoe, Tessa Kate, Skylar, Magnolia, Clementine, Agatha, Chloe, Caleb, Sawyer, Michaela, RoseMarie, Allison, Jack, Jude, Cameron, Alex, Marcus, Lucien, Maezie, Isadora, Wesley, Bennie, Emmeline, Lila, Amelia, Iris, Kaia, Lexi, Mason, Lilyana, and Katie.

Thank you to my fierce posse, my village, my people— you inspire me every day. You know who you are, and I am grateful for you daily.

Thank you to my family. My brother, who is my hero, and my parents, who are the greatest people on this planet.

Made in the USA
San Bernardino, CA
12 May 2020